TWO POINT TWO

ASHUTOSH KUMAR

INDIA • SINGAPORE • MALAYSIA

ISBN
Paperback 979-8-89415-384-1
Hardcase 979-8-89475-976-0

To 14 DTW Waale, who helped me survive
the four years at IIT Kharagpur
and
Aarini and Aarti, who revived
my storytelling spirit.

CHAPTER ONE

Dedicated to the Service of the Nation

The letters, lit in red-neon, on the facade of the main academic building of IIT Kharagpur had a purpose: to remind the students of their duties every time they entered the hallowed portals of the college.

But something was amiss today. The vertical line of the letter 't' in the word 'Nation' was half-lit, making it look like 'Na+ ion.'

Sodium ion!

Someone fresh out of the great Indian ordeal of JEE would have flashbacks.

But not the ones who were stargazing on the Insti top – the roof of the building. For the last two and a half years had wiped their gruelling memories of the JEE. They were now KGPians, the proud residents of IIT KGP!

Ada, Darsh, and Abhik had sneaked in through a broken window on the third floor of the building. It was the first time for Ada. Darsh and Abhik were veterans. In fact, it was a ritual for Darsh to be here on this day every year. On his birthday.

"Why on earth do you like to be here? On your birthday? On the Insti top?" asked a curious Ada, with a slight hint of irritation.

Darsh was lost, his unblinking eyes gazing at the tower rising out of the building. The watchtower. It was a replica of the tower at the old Hijli building, the birthplace of IIT KGP. The tower, he believed, lent the main building its true character. He often dreamt of climbing up the tower and soaking in the breathtaking view of the campus. Grandeur is what he would embrace any moment. His physique, to a good extent, had already embraced it. A body, shy of six feet, toned by swimming, and a face with sharp, angular features, lending him a sculpted appearance. His presence commanded attention, like the watchtower.

"This is the only way he can be at the top of his class," quipped Abhik, pointing below where the classes ran.

Ada let out a guffaw. The silence of the night was punctured, distracting Darsh.

Darsh hushed her. "Shh...Supercop Jha will come!"

Supercop Jha was a living legend on the campus. The tall, lean-framed, and striking chief of campus security. Adored by the students for his oiled moustache and the smile behind it.

Ada feigned anger. "Fine! So, answer my question. Why this place for your birthday?"

"No idea. I just love this place. Somehow it makes me feel unique. Besides, I can get a good view of our 2.2," replied Darsh in a deep resonant voice, his eyes staring into the distance.

All eyes followed Darsh's.

2.2. The central circuit road in the campus, which was 2.2 kilometres in length. Most of the major spots of the campus were located on either side of the road. But, to the inhabitants of the campus, it was more than just a road.

"Imagine all those giants who cycled on this road," continued Darsh, "rushing to attend their classes, their slipper-worn feet pedalling with all their might, others jumping on their carriers. Vinod Gupta, Arjun Malhotra, Ajit Jain…"

"Ashok Khemka, Arvind Kejriwal," cut in Abhik.

"Of course! How can we forget those activist-idols of yours?" Darsh's voice carried a hint of tease.

"Not activists. Flag-bearers of truth!" retorted Abhik.

"Not again guys," intervened Ada. "What's the plan for the celebration? Start with GPL?" She looked at Abhik, waggling her eyebrows.

GPL was a celebratory ritual where the birthday boy's buttocks received a generous dose of direct kicks or slipper slaps. Sometimes the slippers were drenched in water for an enhanced experience.

Whether the girls performed this ritual was a mystery to the boys. They obviously were aware, Ada just established that.

"Come on guys, I had my share of GPL at the hall," protested Darsh. Abhik nodded in support. Both were from the same hall of residence or hostel. "Besides, I have to leave now. Halwai must be waiting for me. If I am late, he will deep fry me."

"Who's Halwai? And it's your birthday today. What's the hurry?" asked Ada, genuinely baffled.

"Let me have the honour to introduce Halwai," announced Abhik, clearing his throat and bringing his right fist closer to his mouth, pretending to hold a microphone. His eyes, sunk a bit in the sockets, beamed with a certain joy. His long hair, parted from the middle, bounced behind his ears, some loose strands touching his eyelids. He raised his left hand, the index finger popping out of the fist and pointing to the sky.

His phone buzzed before he could even begin. 'Saad' flashed on his phone. He had to take the call.

"Where the hell are you *ch…?*" Abhik stopped shy of hurling a cuss word. Saad was very sensitive to swear words, and Abhik respected that. He moved closer to the broken window, giving instructions to Saad on the phone.

"Now tell me, why can't you spend time with us?" asked Ada, looking into Darsh's eyes. The passion in her eyes was palpable. Her hands reached for his, her slender fingers warmly covering the back of his palm.

He took a deep breath. "Look Ada, the Gymkhana elections are hardly 2 months away. And you know that I will be contesting for the post of the VP. My seniors are hell-bent on winning this time. It has been more than five years since our hall…"

"You and your poltu!" she interjected. Politics became *poltu* at IIT KGP. "I sometimes wonder. Are we here for poltu or to study? So many bright minds, wasting their time. For what? Do you think all your giants…"

"I know, I know," he interrupted her, his voice a notch higher. "But this is what I aspired to. Always. This is my choice. I may not go for M.Tech or PhD, and do some breakthrough innovation for the country. But I still can do many other things. And become a giant…" With a mischievous twinkle in his eyes, he continued, "Besides, it has its own rewards. Imagine if I become the VP, you will become the first lady of the campus. Eh?"

He beamed, his smile carrying a hint of condescension. Instinctively, he started caressing her fingers.

She jerked his hands away.

"Huh! You, Mr. Darsh Agarwal, become whatever you want. I will be only Ada Chavan. No first, second, third… lady!"

Her serious tone caused a sudden lull. And then, as if on cue, both burst into laughter.

"Folks, I have to bring Saad up." Abhik's voice startled them. "I will be back in a minute. Till then please use your time for PDA."

Before Ada could react, Abhik disappeared.

"How can someone be so *fattu*, he can't even come here on his own! It's just a matter of taking a few flights of stairs and sneaking through the window." Darsh had never been kind to Saad.

Ada registered her disgust. "That's mean, Darsh! Not everyone is as daring, as ambitious, as aspiring, as you are."

He puffed up his chest. After a cinematic pause, he proclaimed, "I know, nobody can match me."

He turned to Ada. Her face was screaming her disbelief at his utterance. She recoiled away.

"Hey, hey, I am just kidding." He pulled her, wrapping his hands around her. Her head snuggled into his chest.

He continued, "You know how much I value this friendship with all of you, how much I love you. What clicked among the 4 of us... what pulled me to you... God knows! But now I can't imagine a world..."

He stopped abruptly as he felt soft tremors and a hint of moistness on his shirt.

"Never be heartless, Darsh!" said Ada, in a quivering voice, without looking up. "I want you to care for others and stand up for them like you did for me. Not like the last VP who…" A surge of memories from within choked her voice.

He mumbled, hugging her tighter. "Yes Ada, that's one thing I have learnt from my father. Never be… selfish."

His last word trailed off as if, despite his best efforts, the word escaped from his hold.

There are moments which have the power to dissolve your past. Both were experiencing such a moment.

"Are you happy with my decision to contest?" he asked softly, bringing her back to the present.

She snatched herself away from him. "Not at all!" she said sternly.

His face drew a blank look. "B…but, you had earlier…"

She broke into laughter. "Look at your face! Of course, I am. You fool! I am very proud."

She stood up, raising her hands as if holding a banner. "When your campaign starts, I will be there with a banner in my hand, standing on the Insti top, shouting, 'Vote for Darsh Agarwal!'"

He chuckled. "You are one damn good actor. Rashi ma'am is totally blessed to have you."

A message popped up on Darsh's phone. He jumped out of his seat as soon as he saw the name of the sender. "I will have to go now. Else, Halwai will kill me tonight!"

Thud. The familiar sound of slippers landing on the roof floor made Ada and Darsh turn their heads towards the broken window. Abhik and Saad were walking up to them.

"Happy Birthday, Darsh!" Saad greeted meekly.

He had a broad face with pockmarks, remnants of a chickenpox episode. His short, curly hair and glasses with a white rim lent him a righteous look. A hint of guilt was perceptible in his voice. He was late for the party as he was occupied at his department lab. But it was not a reason he felt proud of sharing.

Darsh hugged Saad unexpectedly, bringing a smile to Ada's face. "Thanks, Saad. But I have to go, man. I will catch up with you later."

Darsh sprinted to the broken window without waiting for a reply.

"Hey Darsh… wait… wait," shouted Abhik. "I have to tell you something… I am launching our news magazine next week." His voice trailed as Darsh went out of sight, reducing to a mumble.

"It's called Awaaz."

Abhik turned to Saad and Ada, expecting them to inquire about his new venture.

But Ada's mind was occupied with a more fundamental question. She asked, "Who's Halwai?"

***

If one wondered how the minds trained in science and mathematics could appreciate the art of politics, one needed to come to IIT KGP. Not only did they appreciate it, but they had also mastered it. The whole of it – the good, the bad, and the ugly!

Halls essentially functioned as political parties sans any ideology. Coalitions formed among these parties, driven by the rapport among the *senior party leaders*. The coalitions agreed upon candidates for various Gymkhana posts. Identified and groomed by the party leaders, these candidates were thrust into the key activities of the campus: Spring Festival, Tech Festival, Inter IIT, and so on. The new voters, the freshers, who lived a life of solitude away from the love and care of seniors, were bribed with promises, including Maggi at the canteen. Once bribed, they voted. However, those living under the parasol of seniors had no *free will*.

Yes, no free will.

The party leaders instructed their hall students to vote for the candidates picked by the coalitions. The size of the coalitions, thus, largely decided the outcomes of the elections. These coalitions became the soul of politics. Liberate the soul, the body would decompose.

A class of people rose to assist the party leaders.

To nourish the soul.

To guide the mortals to the divinity of politics.

They were omnipresent, omniscient, and omnicompetent, if not omnipotent. They were poltu Gods. Every hall had a bunch of their own Gods. And the stature of a God was inversely proportional to his or her grades.

But soon the winds of change swept over politics. The mortals demanded their free will. The soul was freed. However, the body didn't decompose. It strengthened. The coalitions continued to be formed, but the students were no more instructed. Even if they were, they didn't follow. Not all poltu Gods found this new order appealing enough. Those who came to terms with it shed their divinity to become mortals. The remaining ones, who had no clue how a mortal functioned, continued in the hope to regain their paradise.

Halwai was one of the remnants.

He was pacing furiously in front of his room in the Patel hall. A white vest adorned his torso, his chest hair peeping out from a tiny hole in the vest. His short stature, with rotund features, belied his aura of authority in the hall. Halwai didn't come from a family of *sweetmeat sellers*, as his nickname suggested. He rather behaved like one, earning him the title. In his torn white vest, he would sit cross-legged and churn endless stories, as any Halwai would do while stirring oil in a cauldron.

He had been waiting for Darsh for the last half hour.

"Don't worry, man! He must be on his way."

A voice, in a sleepy tone, came from Halwai's room. What followed were wisps of smoke. Chimney, as he was called, was another remnant. A six-foot-two-inches lanky figure, with hair brushed back neatly and squinted sleepy eyes, Chimney was quite opposite to Halwai. His walk, his speech, his demeanour carried an air of carelessness. *Peace maaru* in IIT KGP lingo. What earned him the title of Chimney is a no-brainer. Standing tall, when he would puff a cigarette, he would look no less than a chimney billowing smoke!

Halwai halted in his march and stormed inside the room. He plucked the smouldering cigarette out of Chimney's lips and tossed it away.

He growled, "*Saale* Chimney, you shut up!"

Chimney didn't take offence; he immediately started looking for another cigarette.

Halwai continued, huffing, "This *chutiya* is riding on a high horse now. We are bloody waiting for him for half an hour. No respect for us, no respect for our time. Maybe we need to remind him that we are still his seniors. Huh!"

Chimney had lit-up another cigarette by now. He said, "It's his birthday, man! Let him enjoy!"

"So what! The elections are hardly two months away. Just because you are a juice doesn't mean that everyone is dying to vote for you. Gone are those days!" Halwai was unforgiving today.

With a face sans hair, Darsh harboured attractive looks. He was a *juice*.

"And do you think I have all the time in the world?" continued Halwai with the same ferocity, "I have to prepare my CV; the placement is going to start soon. All this romance with Ada. I am telling you… The kind of ruckus she created last year, sucking Darsh into that. And all that noise, for what? Just a small incident. I need to really warn him to stay away from her."

Halwai balled his fist and punched it into his other palm. He never approved of the relationship between Darsh and Ada. Not because he himself had no girlfriend. Because he saw petty affairs like romance as a mere hindrance to the noble pursuit of power.

Chimney tried to divert Halwai. "Leave it, man. Let's talk about the campaign. What needs to be done? Tell me."

Halwai took a long breath, and then let it out in a rush. "Yes, no point in wasting time. Look, we need to build an image for Darsh. An affable, down-to-earth image, with stellar achievements. Right now, he is seen as a very flashy and loud guy. Last year, in SF, he got drunk and went on the stage, gyrating his hips like Shakira. And throwing flying kisses at the audience." SF was short for Spring Festival, the annual social and cultural festival of IIT KGP.

"Hmm… good point. How can we do that? He has all the credentials. He is in the core team of SF, so he can bring sponsorships…"

Halwai cut Chimney short, "Don't forget his main opponent is already in Gymkhana. And Darsh has never been to Gymkhana."

Chimney gave a quizzical look. *"Who's this?"*

"*Abe chutiye*. Mahe. He is currently the G.Sec, Sports. General Secretary," yelled Halwai, emphasising the last two words. "He is lobbying hard to build a brand-new gym. His preparations for the Inter IIT Sports look perfect. An absolutely good material for VP. How will Darsh stand against him? Only by bringing sponsorship for SF? Huh… we need to do something about Mahe."

"And what about the other one? There is one more candidate, right?"

"No chance. He is useless. By just becoming a placement coordinator…"

Bang!

Halwai was interrupted by the door slamming open. Darsh was standing there, panting. He could see rage in Halwai's eyes and a skewed smile on Chimney's face. The visuals of the OP days flashed before him.

***

"Now you know who's Halwai!" Abhik tried to gauge Ada's reaction.

Ada shrugged her shoulders. "Yes. And no. These poltu Gods are impossible to fathom. Anyway, I also need to leave now. It's past 12. I will have to come up with an excuse for our beloved Security Didi."

The girls' hostel, Sarojini Naidu hall or SN, didn't allow the girls to be out after ten at night. Security Didi ensured that the rule was followed. But the girls had their ways.

"Hey Ada, I have an idea. Let's take a round of the 2.2. After all, it's Darsh's birthday. And he loves 2.2," proposed Abhik.

The three of them had started walking towards the broken window by now.

"That's right. Except that the birthday boy himself is not here," came the reply from Ada.

"But we have you, the half of *Adarsh*!" quipped Abhik, a big grin on his face. He deliberately used the word, now popular on the campus.

Ada punched Abhik in feigned anger. "I just hate that word. It's so stupid!"

She then turned to Saad. "You never dare speak that word."

"Of course. I also hate this word," said Saad. And he was honest. "But can we go for a stroll on 2.2... Please?"

"Fine. It's only because you are asking, Saad. Not because of you, Abhik."

Abhik grinned. He couldn't help but notice the glint in Saad's eyes.

***

The 2.2 was abuzz with night-wanderers.

Content couples, walking with their fingers enmeshed. Steadfast students, coming back from or heading to labs. Delirious drunks, heading outside the campus for their next shot. Frustrated *facchas* or freshers, planning to change their departments or reappear for JEE to improve their rank. Starved souls, rushing to grab a bite at night food canteens after skipping their dinner at the mess. Careless characters, oblivious of tomorrow's exam.

If someone turned the emotions of these wanderers into road breakers, driving on the 2.2 would be one hell of a ride. And hell, it was!

Ada, Abhik, and Saad were taking a turn from the IIT main road to Nalini Ranjan Sarkar Avenue road, which was parallel to Scholar's Avenue road. Together, these three roads constituted 2.2.

"I am a little scared about the Computer Software course. I know the Prof is cool, but it's going over my head." Ada knew this was a course common to the three of them, so she brought up the topic.

"*Peace maaro*! Saad is there," announced Abhik. "Do you know how much he scored in the last surprise test? 19 out of 20. Hell, that was a surprise test. I am sure the Prof himself was surprised. And his notes?

Maa kasam, pure gold. Even if the Prof comes across them, he will wonder when did he teach so much. Isn't it, Saad?"

Abhik threw his hand around Saad's shoulder.

Before Saad could respond, Ada jumped in, "I know. Thank you, Saad, for being in my life. Otherwise, these two stooges were just ruining it."

Ada gave a friendly pat on Saad's arm. The blush on his face went unnoticed.

It was time for Saad to respond to all the flattery. "Folks, you will have my notes. No need to butter me up! However, I will not give my original notes this time. Please make a photocopy. Last time, after a two-day hunt, I found my own notes lying on a messy table in my own hall. Painted with fish curry!" The memory of the curry-painted papers flashed before him, making him shudder.

Abhik proudly said, "You Azad hall guys are so pathetic. Look at us, the Patelians!"

"Abhik, in case you forgot, I had given you the notes. From you it went to Darsh, and then God knows who. And finally, it landed at our mess table."

"Ah! The circle of life!" smiled Abhik sheepishly.

Ada pointed to the newly built guest house. "I don't know what's our fascination with this word. Tech. Look at this new guest house, they have named it Tech Guest House. We already have Tech societies, Tech Gymkhana, Tech market, Tech hospital."

"Ten years, hence, when the world will go tech, then it will remember us as the pioneers," prophesied Abhik.

"Oh! my oracle, why don't you rename your news magazine to Tech Awaaz?" asked Ada.

"But there is nothing tech about it!" protested Abhik.

"That's exactly my point!" said Ada emphatically.

Saad chuckled.

The yellow stone proclaiming 'Patel Hall of Residence' was in sight. It stood at the entrance of the PAN loop—a circuit road connecting Patel, Azad, and Nehru halls. They constituted the senior halls. Others among them were Radha Krishnan (RK), Rajendra Prasad (RP), and Lala Lajpat Rai (LLR or Lallu). After savouring the first year of freedom and solitude in Meghnad Saha (MS) and Homi Jahangir Bhabha (HJB) halls, the students moved to the senior halls in their second year, when they had to undergo an 'orientation programme' or OP, an endearing term for ragging. Over time, new halls were added, responding to the increasing strength of the institute.

While every hall fiercely competed against others, the word ferocity donned a new meaning in the PAN loop. Especially in the Patel hall. The first thing that the new residents learnt from their seniors was that their worthiness would not be assessed by the number of medals they earned, but rather by the number of bones they fractured on the sports ground!

"You know what was the first thing we learnt in our first year from our seniors?" said Ada, staring in the direction of the PAN loop. Abhik and Saad waited for something profound. "Stay away from the PAN loop!"

The profundity hit Abhik and Saad.

After a pause, Ada continued, "Little did I know that I had to also stay away from..."

She couldn't complete her sentence. The moistness in her eyes, carrying a hint of anger, glinted in the street light.

"And look, how seriously you followed the advice. Forget that your best friends are from the PAN loop, you have even made your *sasural* in Patel!" remarked Abhik, with a naughty twinkle in his eyes.

A fleeting smile crossed Ada's lips. Abhik's remark delivered its purpose.

Ada mounted her bicycle. She felt she wouldn't be able to contain herself for long.

"I have to leave now. See you later. And Abhik, for your silly remark, you will have to treat me at Eggies."

She didn't wait for Abhik to respond. She rode into the darkness, punctuated by the street lights on the Scholar's Avenue road. Her fading silhouette outlined her athletic body.

A body which concealed a deeply scarred heart.

The tennis court on the left was bathed in floodlights, but forlorn. Ada felt attracted to it, she slowed down. A sense of grief soothed her. Someone joined her from behind. At first startled, she smiled upon seeing the face.

It was Amrita, a second year.

***

Ada and Amrita entered the SN Hall gate, crossing a couple standing under the PMT.

Piya Milan Tree was an iconic tree, where the parched love birds of the campus perched. You would enter an elite club if you were seen with a girl at the PMT. Soon you would become the talk of the campus and, if lucky enough, you would find a mention in the wall-magazine Junk, which, true to its name, nobody read.

Ada and Darsh became *Adarsh* after being spotted under the PMT.

She clearly remembered the first time she met him at the tree. She was in a white T-shirt, an image of a dancing Shiva printed on it, and black jeans. He was in formal attire—white shirt and black trousers. He was coming straight from an interview at the Gymkhana for the SF team, a stepping stone to his political journey. They had initially decided to meet under the GMT, General Meeting Tree. It was another tree reserved for mundane activities, like the exchange of study notes. An apt place, given that they didn't feel like a couple yet, even though they had been meeting frequently now. But today was different!

A sweet desire rose within her. To express her feelings. To turn into a couple.

She came early and went to stand at the PMT. He came, riding on his bicycle, and stopped at the GMT. A few metres away, both stood still. Like two magnetic poles feeling the pull, but not enough to run towards each other. Knowing the repercussions of standing under the PMT, he threw a baffled look at her. She returned a smile. A few moments passed, laden with anticipation. His fingers curled firmly on the handles of his bicycle; its wheels came to life. He started walking the proverbial extra mile. With every step, his heartbeat grew louder, but feet lighter. The magnetism was at play now.

"*Why here*?" was all he could ask when he reached her. "*Just like that*," was the answer.

The memory turned into a smile on Ada's face, which didn't go unnoticed by Amrita and Security Didi.

"He…hello Didi!" fumbled Ada, coming back to reality. "All good with you?"

"Yes. And I can see you are good, too!"

Didi was in a jovial mood. Otherwise, by this time, questioning all the latecomers, listening to their fairly elaborate excuses, and warning them, she was almost dead. With Ada, she had developed a special relationship over the last year. A relationship where all the late-night entries by Ada went unquestioned by Didi for a brief period, and where Ada could sometimes cry in front of her without being judged or advised.

"By the way, why are you so late, girl?" asked Didi, turning to Amrita, who still had no blessings from Didi. It was believed that you had her blessings once she started calling you by your name.

Ada jumped in, "She was with me, for a rehearsal. Don't worry, Didi!"

Amrita had requested Ada to cover for her. Ada didn't bother to ask her where she actually was. Amrita hurried away without waiting for Didi to react.

"What, Ada! Why do you keep covering for others?" frowned Didi.

"Let it be, Didi. She was just enjoy…"

Ada stopped midway. Her pupils dilated, staring at the approaching figure behind Didi. Her facial muscles tensed, her body became stiff, her chest heaved visibly.

After a few moments, when she gained her composure, she could only say, "I need to catch some sleep. Good night, Didi."

She left, leaving Didi perplexed. When Didi turned back to bid her goodnight, she understood what made her leave in such a hurry.

Sheetal was standing there.

CHAPTER TWO

The Nehru canteen was busy feeding the bodies that rebelled against the dinner served in the mess and the minds that rebelled against the sunrise. Named after its owner, Asim's was famous for its cheese Chotai sandwich and Bhatu Maggi, and for bringing the students of the PAN loop together.

"I am not sure, Yousuf, whether this is a good idea. Besides, it would be too time-consuming." Abhik gulped down some of his words with a slurp of his Bhatu Maggi.

Abhik and Yousuf ran a blog, titled 'Once Upon a News!' which had about three hundred subscribers.

Rarely spotted on the campus, Yousuf loved to sit for hours behind his computer either coding or writing for the blog. One place where he was found with a sincere regularity was at Banjara, a theatre group run by a maverick on the campus. Theatre nourished his carefree soul. When Abhik started the blog, Yousuf was one of the early subscribers. What led him to join Abhik was the honesty and idealism with which the latter was running it.

Yousuf was waiting for his 'half-fry double side.' The simplicity of the name belied the complexity with which he instructed the cook in the kitchen. The eggs had to be flipped on the other side only after the yellow on one side achieved a crusty veneer while the white achieved a half-fried status. Naming it after its creator, the dish might soon find a place on the menu of Asim's. Like Bhatu Maggi did.

"Time-consuming?" gasped Yousuf, incredulously. "Do you have any idea how much time we are spending right now on our blog, in analysing all the news from all over India? And for what? Three hundred and four subscribers! The number has not moved an inch in the last month. I understand it takes time, but how much? We are not here for eternity! What I am proposing is to move beyond this analysis shit."

Yousuf's dish arrived. Suspiciously, he poked it with a fork first. Then, neatly cutting a bite out of it, he placed it in his mouth. "Umm." He produced a sound of satisfaction while chewing the bite. And then he devoured his half-fry double side.

Abhik tried to argue, "But Yousuf, why do you want to just write for a small audience…"

A bunch of papers slapped against a nearby table distracted Abhik. From the sound of it, one could easily guess the anger or disgust of the person who tossed the papers. Abhik's ears pricked up when he heard 'Schol's Av.' Scholar's Avenue was an existing newsmagazine of the campus.

The angry young man rambled. "You call this rubbish a news magazine! I call it Junk Part Two, or better Junk Returns. Look at the kind of stories covered. Who are the guest singers at the Spring Fest, how many colleges are participating in the Spring fest, which are the hotspots to make out with a girl in the Spring Fest? As if one lives on the campus only for the Spring Fest. The paper is full of stories on what is still more than a month away. What is happening now, what is a pain in our ass now gets no mention. The mess fees are increased, for serving us rubbish every day. The BC Roy hospital looks like it will crumble tomorrow. The bully professors have made our lives hell. You remember the Ada incident, how poorly they covered it. I wish someone could write about the real issues on this campus, take on the administration."

"This is precisely why I want to write for this small audience," said Yousuf animatedly, thanking the angry young man in his heart. "This small audience will care for every word we write. Because we will be writing about their issues, their pain, their problems, the injustice they face. Unlike writing about a bunch of national issues, which rarely anyone cares about."

Abhik closed his eyes briefly, sliding into a monk-like silence. Pain. Problems. Injustice. He could hear these words repeating themselves. In a snap, he opened his eyes. And looked into Yousuf's eyes.

"What should be the name of our magazine?"

Yousuf's eyes widened in delight. He had already thought of a name.

"We will be the voice of KGP. We will be Awaaz."

"We will be Awaaz." The four words rang in Abhik's ears, as he climbed the stairs of Vikramshila, leading to

the foyer. Draped in the whiteness of the moonlight, Vikramshila was a newly built academic building.

The Awaaz team was waiting for Abhik at the foyer. So were the printed copies of the first edition. It took almost two months for him and Yousuf to give birth to Awaaz—raising sponsorships, building a team of editors and reporters and graphic designers, designing a layout, and finally deciding the content for the first edition. The birth pangs would soon turn into tears of joy at the sight of the newborn, at the smell of the newborn.

The foyer echoed with claps when Abhik came into sight. Yousuf waved a copy of the newsmagazine at him.

The sight of the newborn.

Both hugged each other. The waft of the fresh print hit Abhik's nostrils.

The smell of the newborn.

Abhik looked at his team, beaming with pride.

"*We are Awaaz.*" He heard himself saying.

Abhik took the stage, the flat space between two flights of stairs. Yousuf stood at the corner of the stage, occasionally catching a glimpse of the full moon. As the Chief Editors, they were supposed to address their team on this momentous occasion.

Abhik started. "Sitting in Asim's two months ago, Yousuf told me, we will be Awaaz. And today we are Awaaz."

The audience cheered his emphatic start. The foyer echoed once again.

"But…" Abhik waited to regain the attention of the audience. "But we still are not the voice of KGP. Just by naming ourselves Awaaz, we can't become the voice. There is an extra mile we all need to travel. Together. To become the voice. Yousuf and I share amazing camaraderie. But that's not what has really brought us so far. It's our disagreements. Disagreements over which story should be chosen. What are the real issues of the students? Which one deserves a place among our eight pages? Disagreements over how the story should be written. How should we research? How should we verify the authenticity of the data we are collecting? Disagreements over choosing our patrons. Many, many disagreements. And I value these disagreements more than our camaraderie. One of my ideals from the world of journalism, Ramnath Goenka, said—*I have committed every crime in the Indian Penal Code, except murder.* And I think disagreeing with others is the crime you can start with today, as a journalist. Remember we are not here only for adding two extra lines to our CVs. We are here to become the voice of KGP. We are here to become Awaaz."

A thunderous applause followed.

"And now it's time for our other Chief Editor, Yousuf." Abhik gestured Yousuf to come over.

The applause continued.

Reluctance was writ large over Yousuf's face.

Initiated by Abhik, everyone started chanting 'Yousuf.' He had no choice.

"First of all, I disagree with Abhik," chuckled Yousuf, bringing a smile to everyone's face. "It's not only our disagreements that have brought us this far. It's all of you who have made this journey possible. And even if you want, you can't disagree with me on this. Secondly, Abhik has committed another crime. He has stolen my speech. So, I have nothing to say now. Thirdly, it's a full moon tonight. So, don't forget to look up."

With a smile that only an enlightened soul can afford, Yousuf walked back to his corner. A moment of silence followed; the silent heads turned up to see the full moon. When enlightenment dawned upon them, a mix of laughter and applause greeted Yousuf. By then, Yousuf was already on his way to meet the first love of his life. Abhik knew where he was headed.

"I will see you at Eggies," shouted Abhik at the top of his lungs before Yousuf disappeared into the building.

***

On the other side of Vikramshila, the full moon was dripping over bodies lying in a supine position, their eyes shut. A tranquil voice was calming their minds, guiding them on a celestial journey. Occasionally, the bodies twitched, their stress finding a vent.

"You have found your star. Slowly, very slowly… land on your star. Feel the surface of the star with the skin of your bare feet. Let the feeling…the sensation pass through your every cell. Slowly, very slowly…the sensation has reached the tip of your nail…the tip of the longest strand of hair on your head."

The voice took a pause, allowing the bodies to feel the sensation.

"You are now ready to expand. You are now expanding. Slowly, very slowly. You have expanded over the entire surface of the star. Don't stop here. You are expanding…expanding…and expanding. Slowly, very slowly. You are expanding over the entire universe. Over every star…over the moon… over the sun…over the earth…over every planet. You have expanded to every atom…every cell of the cosmos. Feel this expansion…in your feet…in your hands…in your head…in your heart…in your mind…in your soul."

Another pause. It was time to bring them back to the terrestrial.

"Now. Slowly, very slowly…bring your awareness back to your body. To your feet. To your hands. To your face. To your forehead. Focus there for some time."

Another pause.

"Now, slowly rub your palms and warm them up. Cup both your eyes with your warm palms. Open your eyes inside the cover of your palms. Slowly, take your palms away. Let the moonlight caress your face, and seep into its every cell. Sit upright. Stay silent for a minute. And just observe."

The figure behind the voice was a soothing comfort to the opening eyes, who were slowly coming to terms with the real world. A supple figure, adorned with kohled eyes and flowing hair, and draped in vibrant colours. Moving with the elegance of a dancer, she was a pure reservoir of energy. Her every step was as firm on the ground as it was ready to take off. The radiance of her smile carried a hint of pride – a pride in who she was and what she would be. If not a thespian, then no one could imagine who Rashi could be!

Rashi, the enigmatic founder of Banjara, introduced real theatre to IIT KGP. Before that, elaborate sets and contorted faces were synonymous with theatre. The dramatics societies, prefixed by 'tech,' were the victims and the perpetrators of shoddy theatre. But theatre is ethereal, theatre is fluid, which allows one to immerse in the joys and sorrows of life, yet be a distant observer – was something she was trying hard to instil into the engineering minds, trained to think in binary. 'Life is a drama,' after all, was the maxim she believed in. Bringing theatre out of the narrow confines of an auditorium, she made the best use of the landscape the campus offered. Soon Banjara had its imprints on the major landmarks of the campus.

"My dear students, now that you are back to this beautiful world, let's talk about our upcoming performance."

Rashi's voice demanded attention from everyone present there.

"I have chosen a play by Sarveshwar Dayal Saxena, it's called Haathi Ki Pon. Here are a few copies of the script. We will perform next month, in January, but the rehearsals have to start now."

A murmur ensued, forcing her to stop midway.

"Okay. What is it? Will someone tell me?" she asked, unable to locate the source of the murmur.

"Placements, Ma'am," a timid voice came.

"What about it?" asked Rashi in a careless tone of voice.

The final year student mustered the courage to reply. "In December, we will be appearing for our job interviews. I don't think we will be able…'

"That's fine! The final years don't need to perform. We have enough performers, I guess."

"Ma'am, but if we plan this slightly later, we will also be able to participate," the student tried to reason.

Others were in awe of the student's courage. It's not always they saw a dinghy challenging a storm.

"Tell me, will you stop watching movies when you appearing for your job interviews? Will you stop going to Eggies or Veggies, whatever it is, with your friends? Will you stop talking to your girlfriend, if you have one?"

She stared blankly at the student, making him fidgety.

"If the answer is no, then you know what would be my response to your request? How do you expect me to stop? Just for your placements?"

Her bluntness cast a silence over the assembly.

"*Banjara* is not for those who want to add extra lines to their CVs. Go join your tech dramatics societies in that case. And become tech actors! Banjara is for those who get goosebumps the moment they step on the stage, who yearn to live infinite lives through their characters, who realise that there is a life beyond chasing a mundane career. I am not against building CVs and scoring good CGPA. But I don't want you to chase them. They should be chasing you. Only then you become a true Banjara, a nomad who doesn't chase but is followed!"

Her breathless spiel led to embarrassed heads, bowing down.

Barring a few who, on the contrary, couldn't take their eyes off her for even a second. Yousuf, Ada, and Saad were among them.

Yousuf's brush with his *first love* happened in his first year. The restless nerd inside him found a caring home in Banjara. Ada's love for Rashi and Banjara didn't happen at first sight. In fact, she found Rashi to be an arrogant character in the beginning, an impression most carry in their first encounter. It's only over time, especially over the last one year, that the love blossomed, soon turning into reverence. You are bound to respect someone with whom you can share your grief as many times as you wish, without being judged. For Saad, who had joined Banjara only a few days back, the love or respect was more for someone else than for theatre or Rashi!

"We will start tomorrow," announced Rashi, peeling off the layer of silence which was growing uneasily over everyone. "Those who will come will be a part of the next performance. And those who can't…"

Leaving her sentence midway, she stood up and collected her bag. With bated breath, everyone waited for her to complete.

"...don't worry. You can join the next performance. The doors of Banjara will be open for you! Always!"

***

An army marches on its stomach.

At IIT KGP, the army, mostly marching in the glow of the moon, was never fed at a singular point. One usually started with the mess at one's hall.

Not privatised yet, the mess system tried its best to live up to its reputation – low quality at high price! What made it worse was the don't-give-a-hoot attitude among the mess workers, ready to go on a strike at the slightest provocation. In the end, one would settle by marking the days when the mess served one's favourite dish.

Marching on, the second point was the private canteen within a hall. These canteens often offered customised dishes, the most popular of them finding a permanent place on the menu.

And finally, a range of eateries within and outside the campus.

Veggies was one of them, at a prime location on the 2.2, in the heart of the campus. It sated the army's appetite. By feeding their growling bellies with fast food. By feeding their curious minds with *bhaat* or useless chat. A section of Veggies became Eggies from 11 pm to 3 am; egg dishes were added to its menu. The waft of the cooking was often accompanied by the melody of old songs, played on Champa's radio.

Champa, the owner of the restaurant, whose claim to fame was that he served the KGPians who are now serving the world. While placing the order, one would often find him talking to these KGPians. Sometimes, he would proudly flash his mobile screen showing a number prefixed by +1. The name, Champa, however, was a misnomer. It belied the masculinity his every gesture conveyed.

"We need to think hard about money to run the show," said Abhik in a contemplative tone, tapping on the black granite top of the table.

After the meeting at Vikramshila, the team dispersed for the distribution of the copies of Awaaz on the campus. Abhik took the responsibility for distribution in his hall. The Chief Editor was not shy of becoming a newspaper hawker! Once done, he headed for Veggies. He was soon joined by Rajat and Dhiru, two editors of Awaaz. Yousuf was awaited.

"We can't simply keep on going with begging bowls every time," continued Abhik, a hint of disgust visible on his face. He suddenly turned to the cashier counter and shouted, "Champa, how long for a simple hot chocolate!" The disgust permeated in his voice.

"Begging bowls? What are you talking about? We are giving advertisements. Real estate in our magazine in return for money. It's a standard practice," protested Dhiru, eliciting a nod from Rajat.

"Dhiru, I understand. And you are right. But what I meant was, we started Awaaz for writing stories. Good, thought-provoking stories. Not to keep running after the advertisers. I hated it in my guts when I had to stand for hours at that computer shop at Puri gate. What's the name of that bloody shop…Info…Some Infotech. Convincing him to put one ad…one small quarter-page ad. And finally, how much did he give? Five thousand. That's it. Peanuts!"

"And how do you propose to raise these peanuts otherwise?" asked Dhiru bluntly.

It didn't sting Abhik. In fact, Abhik appreciated it when someone challenged him.

"I don't know," shrugged Abhik. "I don't have any answer. But that's where we need to put our minds together. All our minds."

Abhik suddenly realised that one mind was absent.

He murmured, "Where the hell is this Yousuf?"

"Dada, your hot chocolate."

A hoarse voice from behind made Abhik turn his head back. His irritation was ready to roll off his tongue. "What the hell? I ordered…" Abhik stopped midway.

The missing mind was there, smiling with a glass of hot chocolate in his hands.

"*Saale* Yousuf, you are coming now!"

"Sorry Dada, it took some time to make your chocolate hot."

A sensuous gesture by Yousuf evoked a guffaw from Dhiru and Rajat. Abhik tried his best to not give in but burst out laughing soon.

Yousuf sat down next to Abhik. A punch landed on Yousuf's stomach; the breath escaped him in a soft groan.

"Sorry folks. I didn't want to be late, but Rashi ma'am was ripping apart a final year," said Yousuf. Her livid face flashed before him.

No one expressed even a hint of surprise. What Yousuf said befitted her image in their heads.

"When was the last uneventful rehearsal with Rashi ma'am? Can you recollect?" Abhik asked Yousuf in all seriousness.

Yousuf searched his memory frantically for an answer despite being fully aware of the futility of the exercise. Suddenly, realising that all eyes were on him, Yousuf jolted himself.

"Leave it folks. Let's go back to what you were discussing before I came."

A sensible suggestion, all nodded their heads.

Dhiru picked up the threads. "How do we run the show? That's what we were talking about. Our Chief Editor here feels advertisement money is like a handout."

Abhik raised his eyebrows. Yousuf shot him a questioning glance.

"That's not really what I meant. I am just asking us to think of better ideas to raise funds, better than convincing these morons who will suck our blood calculating their returns!" Abhik raised his finger to do air quotes around his last word.

"I have an idea, a better one," said Rajat. A man of few words, but when he spoke it was worth listening to.

"Rajat! Where were you till now? Go ahead, we are all ears!" exclaimed Yousuf, pecking a kiss on Rajat's forehead only to be wiped instantly by the latter, and receiving a disgusted look in return.

Rajat laid out his idea. "I know professor Tiwari very well. He is the HOD of the HSS department. Humanities and Social Sciences. He is a die-hard promoter of the Hindi language. He can be easily convinced to fund Awaaz from his department. All in the name of promoting Hindi! We can create an honorary position for him at Awaaz to massage his ego. I am telling you, if we play this right, we will be set for the next couple of years."

Not an eyelid batted.

"*Phodu!*" yelled Yousuf in excitement. *Genius*.

Rajat beamed. Dhiru gave his nod of approval. Abhik didn't look convinced.

Abhik looked into Rajat's eyes. "I appreciate your idea. But I doubt this will work. Remember, we will be writing against the administration. In fact, our current editorial attacks the hike in the mess fees. But I guess this attack is benign enough to punish a toddler that is Awaaz. But imagine, what will happen tomorrow when we write more on such issues, targeting the administration? How long will they be silent? One day you will get a summon from, maybe Prof Tiwari or maybe the Diro himself."

Yousuf jumped from his seat. "Stop Abhik, stop scaring us! By the name of the Director. We will see when that comes. We will say no to their funds then."

"But by then, you would have already taken and spent their funds." Abhik was now staring at Yousuf.

"So, what do you want? We don't go to advertisers because that's begging for you. We don't ask the institute to fund us because then we will not be true to your moral standards of journalism. Why don't you suggest something then? At least Rajat here is giving some ideas," burst Yousuf. The passion in his voice was palpable.

Rajat's phone, lying on the table, beeped. He picked it up to see the message. And then he furiously typed the reply. Once he hit the send button, he looked at Yousuf and Dhiru, avoiding Abhik altogether. "Hey, sorry folks but I have to catch up with someone at Chedi's. Let me know if this idea is good with you. And I can pursue it."

Rajat abruptly stood up, and started walking towards his bicycle, parked outside the restaurant, without looking back. Clenching his fist tightly around his bicycle keys, he felt a surge of indignation within him.

Chutiya, he muttered under his breath.

***

Chedi's was an institution in itself. An institution that anchored the lives of KGPians.

In essence, it was a roadside eatery, just outside the campus, housed in a ramshackle establishment. It made the KGPians, living in a perpetual state of abject penury, feel royal. The warmth and generosity of Anwar Khan, or Chedi, the owner, extended in the form of a credit roster, khata. Served under the silvery light of the moon, Chedi's food was no less than gourmet. And Chedi's no less than a fine dining restaurant! It was the oldest adda IIT KGP had. Be it the Gymkhana elections, or the next performance by a tech society, or a fakka, an F-grade, in a subject, or treat after OP, or the next hot movie or series – no topic or no occasion had skipped this place.

If the institute was the strict father, Chedi's was the caring mother.

"Shahrukh, one Mohile, one Tinku and two chai!"

Sabu's booming voice was easily recognised by the waiters at Chedi's.

A tall, sturdy, and muscular physique earned him the nickname Sabu, a famous character from an Indian comic book. He was a poltu God from RP Hall. He was sitting across another RPian, one year junior to him. It was a little unusual for a senior to be with a junior at 3 am at Chedi's. Only politics could make this possible.

Sabu had called Rajat to seek his help for their VP candidate. Little did Sabu know that Rajat himself would offer his help.

"C'mon Rajat! It's fine. They don't care about your ideas, they are too full of themselves."

Sabu placed his heavy hands on Rajat's shoulders, dislodging the latter from his chair momentarily.

It was as if Rajat was waiting for this invocation. His pent-up anger burst forth.

"No, Sabu. It's not fine at all. They need to be taught a lesson. I have also given my time to build Awaaz. No less than what they have given. You know,

I was the first one to join them. Even before Dhiru. I understand it was their idea, they deserve to be the Chief Editors. But at least they could have acknowledged my contribution before the team? They could have also invited me for a short address. I would have been far better than Yousuf. *Don't forget to look up at the full moon.* What was he smoking? This idea of raising funds from the HSS department. I had shared it long back with both of them. I did it today with a hope that...that they would have come to their senses. At least Yousuf was supportive this time. But this chutiya Abhik. *I and my ethical journalism.* What does he think we are? Corrupt morons? No...no...I need to teach them a lesson. I will quit. Only then they will understand my importance."

"No...no...don't quit. There are a hundred other ways of teaching them a lesson." Sabu again placed his hands on Rajat's shoulders, this time pressing harder. Rajat's shoulder muscles would have ruptured had Shahrukh not announced the arrival of the order.

The gourmet dishes, Mohile and Tinku, were served along with piping hot tea. As the legend goes, both the dishes were concocted by one student, Dhananjay Mohile, in the 1980s. Quite a larger-than-life character, he loved the campus so much that he decided to hang there for a couple of years more than a student would usually spend. In those love-filled years, he probably first invented Mohile – greasy buns sandwiching two double fry eggs, sprinkled with a special masala. Then, probably unsatisfied with his own creation, he concocted a variant, naming it Tinku, after his pet name from home. Mohile and Tinku both immortalised him at IIT KGP.

"Shahrukh, please bring one Wills Navy Cut from Chunnu." Rajat handed over a 10-rupee note to Shahrukh. Having tea without a cigarette was a sin for Rajat. He turned to Sabu. "Yes, go on, Sabu."

Sabu seemed to be lost.

Rajat tried to startle him. "Hey, Sabu!"

Coming out of his reverie, Sabu asked, "Why do you always have a sutta with chai?" He was a non-smoker, uninitiated to the potent combination of cigarette and tea.

"Well, because…both go together…both are meant to be together." Rajat seemed to be at a loss for words. He was never asked such a question.

Sabu grinned weirdly. "And what if I separate the two?"

Rajat couldn't understand where it was going. Shahrukh came to his rescue again, passing on a lit cigarette to Rajat. Before Rajat could act, Sabu snatched the cigarette from Shahrukh's fingers.

Sabu raised the cigarette, held between his thumb and index finger. His grin got wider. And weirder.

"Now, this is your Abhik," proclaimed Sabu, looking at the cigarette. He raised a cup of tea. "And this is your Yousuf." He brought both, the cigarette and tea, closer to each other. "Together, these two are the foundation of Awaaz."

His grin turned into an evil laugh, loud enough for Shahrukh to retreat.

Rajat grimaced, looking at his smouldering cigarette, mentally calculating how many puffs he missed.

"You don't need to quit, Rajat," said Sabu, taking a pause from his laughter. "If you want to teach them a lesson, a real lesson, just smash the foundation." He started moving his raised hands away from each other. "And the best way to do that is…"

He took a cinematic pause, his soul-penetrating gaze meeting Rajat's eyes, his hands frozen in the air.

And then like a true devotee, it flashed to Rajat what God was going to demonstrate. But before he could act to save his cigarette, its smouldering end was kissing the earth. A heartbeat skipped him. He leaped at the soiled cigarette and picked it up.

Dusting off his cigarette, Rajat stared at Sabu's face. "Okay, no graphical explanation please. Just come to the point."

A sip of the tea, followed by a puff of the cigarette, made Rajat let out a sigh of bliss.

"Crush Abhik. Awaaz will crumble, and you will teach them a lesson," growled Sabu.

"But how?"

"Attack at his weakness."

"What do you mean?"

"If ethics are what Abhik can't compromise with, let him commit an unethical act."

"Not possible."

"When I can come to KGP from a place like Bihar Sharif, anything is possible, my dear."

Sabu had many times recounted his story of growing up in a village in Bihar Sharif, where forget the IIT, even engineering was not heard within fifty kilometres of his existence. A chance encounter with the founder of Super 30 changed his life forever, eventually landing him at IIT KGP.

Sabu continued, "You know Mahe is contesting against Darsh. And Darsh is a chaddi-buddy of Abhik. You would be able to kill two birds with one stone – teach them a lesson, and make your hall victorious!"

Rajat's eyes widened with curiosity.

CHAPTER THREE

D-324. A triple room on the second floor of D-wing in Patel hall. DTW or D Top West.

Abhik had called Yousuf, Rajat and Dhiru to his room to discuss the next edition of Awaaz, while his roommate was away. The first edition had seen an enthusiastic response from the student community. While the report on the hike in the mess fees had received applause from the students, it had irked the administration slightly. The Orkut page of Awaaz was brimming with comments. Yousuf was constantly checking the page on the computer of Abhik's roommate.

"Finally, there is a challenger to the age-old guardian of mediocrity. Hail to Awaaz! Ha…ha…you know who has written this comment?" A euphoric Yousuf asked.

"Who?" asked Dhiru.

"Sumit. He was one of the editors at Schol's Av, who quit a few weeks ago, complaining about the falling standards of the magazine. And here is he, with his gracious comment for Awaaz," said Yousuf, taking a screenshot of the comment. He had a plan to include all such comments in the next edition, in a section titled *We heard you!*

"Okay, folks. Enough of massaging your egos with these comments. Back to work. We have to finalise the stories for the next edition," rasped Abhik, without looking away from the screen of his computer.

He had been typing a list of possible stories for the next edition. A book was lying next to his keyboard, titled *If You Are Afraid Of Heights*. The author's name was Rajkamal Jha, an illustrious alumnus of IIT KGP, whom Abhik idolised.

"One last comment," shouted Yousuf, springing out of his chair. Its metal legs screeched against the floor, forcing Abhik to look at him. "Just one. It says, the main story could have sounded better and authentic had the HMC officials commented. Without that it sounds like a concocted story."

The story on the mess fees didn't include any comments from the officials of the *Hall Management Committee*.

"I knew it. I knew it." Abhik pounded on the table with the bottom of his fist. "It was missing, and it was so glaring. I did try to reach out to them. But did I try enough? Don't know." Within a few seconds, his roused passion turned into a dejected look.

Yousuf consoled him. "It's alright, Abhik. It was our first time."

"Yes. And this should be our last time. Next time, no stories without talking to the concerned parties. That should be our rule."

A silence followed Abhik's order.

"Aye, aye Sir!" saluted Yousuf, clicking his heels.

Dhiru and Rajat followed the act. All of them burst out laughing.

"By the way, do you know whose comment it was?" Yousuf had an impish smile on his face.

Knock, knock. The age-old green door protested the knocks by creaking a little, drawing everyone's attention. Yousuf unlatched the door. It was Darsh.

"Wow! Is this what your success party looks like?" boomed Darsh.

Abhik quipped, "Well, we don't have the blessings of sponsors or Gymkhana yet. Like SF!"

His repartee evoked a lopsided smile from Darsh. *How insipid our friendship would be without this banter,* Darsh thought. Abhik, as if he read Darsh's mind, gave a reassuring smile.

"And by the way, we are not partying yet! We were planning for our next edition." Abhik pointed to his open laptop.

"Then, it's the perfect time that I am here!" declared Darsh. "By the way, first edition of Awaaz rocks, that story on the mess fees was superb. Great work guys!"

He, on an impulse, patted Abhik's back.

"Not everyone thinks so. Especially someone… close to you," said Yousuf, raising the suspense in the room. "Ada feels that the story, without any comment from the HMC, sounded like a concocted one."

"Fine. That's right…I mean that's a personal opinion. I personally think…the story was great. But yes…yes, a comment from the HMC would have made it more authentic," said Darsh, fumbling on his way.

"Don't worry Darsh! We are not going to tell her that you disliked her comment." Abhik didn't want to miss any opportunity to tease Darsh. Like he did with Ada.

"I don't really care," said Darsh, ignoring the suppressed smiles in the room. "I came here to help you guys with an explosive story. Now, can we discuss that if we are done with the pleasantries?"

Abhik nodded. The other three adopted an alert posture.

"You know Jena? The Place Com?" asked Darsh. He waited for everyone to give a nod. "He is favouring students from his hall."

The four listeners tried to grasp the gravity of what Darsh just said. The placement process at IIT KGP was overseen by the Career Development Centre, or CDC in short. It was chaired by a handful of professors, and managed by a body of students, who constituted the Placement Committee. The members were called Place Com. Among other tasks entrusted to the committee, one was to verify the CVs of the students appearing for the placement.

"And I have proof," said Darsh resolutely. "You go and see the list of the shortlisted candidates on the notice board. You see the number of students from his hall. And you see the number from other halls. You will understand. Firstly, he is not verifying the CVs coming from his hall at all. Secondly, he is somehow, and I don't know how, getting access to the aptitude test questions of the companies and sharing them with his hall students. That's how the list is full of his students."

"But why don't you complain to the CDC profs?" Dhiru put a brake on Darsh's tirade.

"You think I didn't try that? I went to meet the CDC Chairperson. He didn't give a hoot to what I said. I honestly don't know why. I did some digging. He is an alumnus of KGP. Of the same hall. Probably...probably that could have led to some deal between the two. Now that's something for you to unearth."

"Alright, Darsh," said Abhik, contemplatively. "Even if we believe what you are saying is right, we need to do our own research. And if the story is right, then why not?"

"Yes, by all means. Do your research. I will also share the evidence I have. Anything for a bigger cause. My only request is to hurry up. We don't have many days left. At least some students will benefit if we are able to get this bastard out of the committee."

"But." Rajat knew what he was going to say next would pique Darsh. But he also knew that it would just be a beginning – the beginning of the plan that Sabu had laid out at Chedi's. "Isn't Jena a potential candidate for the VP, and hence your potential opponent?"

"What does that mean?" a startled Darsh asked as if he was caught red-handed.

Rajat explained, "That means that if the story is out, Jena's image goes for a toss, and he is out of the race. One down, one more to go."

He turned to Abhik. "Sorry for raising this. But after all, we are not here to support friends; we are here for responsible journalism."

Darsh stood up, trying hard to contain his rage. "Listen, Rajat, I completely respect your principles. And I would be the last person to get in your way. But my question is this. Even if I have my personal agenda in this story, would you not publish this? After confirming its veracity?"

"Of course, we will," said Rajat in a mollifying tone. "Hey, Darsh, no offence. We know you are a good friend to Abhik, that's why you are here, trying to help him, and us. But I just thought we should be clear… about your intention. It matters. Isn't it, Abhik?"

Rajat turned to Abhik, who was still trying to comprehend what transpired in the last few minutes.

Before Abhik could respond, Darsh was headed to the door.

"I will come back tomorrow with some real proof. Then I leave it up to all of you to decide. As I said, anything for a bigger cause. Bye, everyone."

Darsh left the room.

Filled with silence.

Filled with buzzing heads.

We are not here to support friends; we are here for responsible journalism. Like a song in a loop, it was playing in those heads. At different pitches in different heads. Only one head was at rest.

Rajat was engrossed in texting about his first victory.

***

The metallic twang of the guitar broke Darsh's chain of thoughts. He was still in the gallery of the D-wing, though at its end. The sound came from Kanwa's room, he realised. In his days of yore, he had made an honest attempt to learn the guitar. Kanwa was his mentor. But then he was subsumed by politics. At least, he reasoned so to himself. A few steps ahead and a melancholic song, in Kumar Sanu's voice, emanated from a room. It was Banu's room. Quite a juxtaposition. How a Kumar Sanu's and Metallica's fan lived, and survived, next to each other was a real wonder!

The melancholy, however, carried Darsh back to his chain of thoughts. His face twisted with anger. At what Rajat said. But he also knew that sometimes one had to swallow pride. *Anything for a bigger cause*, he found himself saying under his breath. The thought, however, that he was trying to manipulate his best friend didn't cross his mind at all. It got buried under the *bigger cause.*

Suddenly realising that he might be late to where he was headed, he started taking big strides.

***

"I am sure it's Sabu, I know him quite well. Otherwise that…that…" Halwai roared, his eyebrows knitting in a visible frown. Darsh had just filled him in with what transpired at Abhik's room.

"Rajat." Darsh filled in.

Darsh couldn't help but notice the swirls of smoke emanating from an incense stick placed on a corner of the computer table. Chimney's absence was felt. Halwai is not that religious type, it struck Darsh. Then why the incense stick, maybe to wash away the sins of Chimney, he chuckled in his mind. His scrutinising eyes met a book lying on the table, titled *Five Point Someone*. The book, by a first-time author, Chetan Bhagat, was a recent rage.

"Yes. Whoever he is. He can't have the brains to say all of this. That Jena would be contesting was still a secret. Only a handful of us knew. Sabu is laying out some big plan, I can smell it. He has a strong candidate."

The furrows in Halwai's brows deepened. He knew Sabu's scheming mind. He had encountered it in the past. Only to be defeated by it.

Darsh got rattled by the mention of his formidable opponent. He asked, "How can we get Mahe out of the way? Do you have anything against him? Like you had against Jena?"

"Not at this point. Neither should we be thinking. We need to focus on you," replied Halwai, staring at Darsh with the fervour of a provoked God. Only to draw a blank from his devotee.

The God took pity on his confused devotee.

"We have been thinking about how to build a down-to-earth image for you. Remember we spoke last time! It seems we have a solution, a good one actually. Leave that to us; we will meet tomorrow for this. Now, I have to prepare my CV!" said Halwai, pointing Darsh to the door.

Darsh looked surprised. It had been almost ten days since the placement started. How can Halwai be preparing his CV now?

Halwai dispelled Darsh's confusion.

"Well, I have a CV. Just need to improve it further. The first ten days have been a whitewash. These, bloody Jena kind of people have rigged the process. Now the second phase, after the winter vacation, is the only hope!"

Darsh understood the secondary motives of Halwai behind pushing the story against Jena so vehemently. After all, God had to take care of himself!

"But two things, Darsh!" boomed Halwai, forcing Darsh to stop at the door. "The story of Jena has to be out, at any cost. How will you do this with your good friend, Abhik, I leave it up to you. I will mail you the proof that I am in possession of. But after that..." He didn't feel the need to complete his sentence.

"Yes, I understand. I will take care of it." Darsh gave a reassuring look, that of a worthy devotee.

"And what's the second thing?" he asked.

"Yes, the second..." Halwai stopped. He realised it's not the right time yet. "Nothing. Leave it. I will tell you later. Can you please close the door tightly, and turn off the light? I need to sleep for some time; today is a bloody night out! Building a good CV is hell of a job!"

Halwai, by now, was spread all over his bed, his frame comfortably fitting in the six by three feet metal bed. Darsh followed the instructions, stepping out quietly.

I will soon have to tell him to stay away from Ada. Halwai thought before the sweetness of incense lulled him to sleep.

***

"Good job, Rajat! You made us proud today!"

Sabu's hand was about to land on Rajat's back. The thought of the ensuing trauma made Rajat stiffen his back, thinking that the stiffness would absorb the impact. But he was acutely wrong. What could have been a low whimper was a loud moan.

"And you have made your hall proud as well," added Mahe, resorting to a time-tested rhetoric that never failed to rouse the impressionable minds. As the elections were coming closer, he was getting better at it.

Rajat beamed, slowly gaining consciousness in his numb back. He did not want to miss the opportunity to bask in his glory. "You should have seen Darsh's face when I accused him. Flush with red! He thought he would come, ask for a favour, and bingo, it will be done!"

"There will be many such moments, Rajat. Don't worry. He doesn't know who he is competing with. I am already a G. Sec, and he is yet to hold any position in the Gymkhana," said Mahe in an aggressive tone, gaining an instant nod from Rajat, but an instant smack on the back of his head from Sabu.

"You also don't know yet who you are competing with," snarled Sabu. "Never underestimate your opponent."

He glared at Mahe, forcing him to bow his head apologetically.

He continued, "Darsh has media power with him. He can sway the opinion of the campus, build and destroy reputations with a flick of his hand. That's what he is trying to do now with Jena. That's what he can do tomorrow with you if our plan fails."

He looked at Rajat, who immediately understood the reference to the plan. Mahe gave a clueless look. He was kept in the dark, for obvious reasons. As a candidate, he was told only what he needed to know. Rest, the Gods would take care.

Sabu continued, "In the end, it will not matter whether he had ever stepped into the Gymkhana. What will matter is what he is doing now, what that bloody Halwai is doing NOW."

Sabu was almost shrieking by now, his wide chest heaving. He knew how dogged Halwai could be. Cloaked in guilt, Mahe was immobile. The memory of Sabu crushing his smouldering cigarette at Chedi's flashed before Rajat.

After allowing some time to cool tempers, Sabu again continued, "Look Mahe, your CV is more impressive than Darsh's. No doubt about that! You have been a G.Sec, an Inter IIT medallist, a nine-pointer. You landed a foreign intern this year, got a budget for a new gym sanctioned, and the list is longer. But…but arrogance is the last thing that should touch you. Believe me, it will cloud you, it will ruin you. Your humility is your weapon. Sharpen it!"

"Yes, Sabu. I got what you are saying. I will be careful," said Mahe in an assuring tone. *I will regain your confidence*, he continued under his breath.

"Hey guys, I have an idea," said Rajat. "Darsh is also into sports, I guess swimming. He has been to Inter IIT, not sure whether he won any medal. But Mahe, being a G. Sec Sports, can do something so that Darsh misses the Inter IIT this year. At least his CV will have one less star!"

He was filled with a sense of pride as soon as he finished sharing his idea. He was making his hall proud.

Sabu nodded his head vehemently in disagreement. "No, no. We will not go into such petty fights. It will suck our energies. We have a plan, remember Rajat. And we just need to execute that. Look buddy, we are relying a lot upon you. Just focus on that plan. Don't waste your brain on such lowly ideas. And believe me, you will also be rewarded in the end!" He glanced at Mahe, and then brought his attention back to Rajat. "I have spoken to Mahe. After Awaaz becomes history, you can start your own magazine. And Mahe will extend you all the support. As the VP. And there will be other perks as well!"

Even though his idea was thrashed, Rajat was not hurt. He was a man on a mission, bringing glory to his hall.

***

"What Rajat said was right. I have been pondering over it," said Abhik while taking a sip of his tea.

He was sitting in the canteen of Patel hall with Yousuf. The contract for the canteen was recently awarded to Anil Da, who earlier used to run a small eatery in the PAN loop. It has been five days since Darsh visited them with the idea of exposing Jena. Soon after that visit, Darsh mailed Abhik the evidence against Jena – email exchange of five students from Jena's hall with him, where the latter had shared aptitude test questions from companies appearing for placement. Abhik's team subsequently scrutinised the email content, and conducted their own research as well. All the evidence so far was against Jena.

"Rajat may be right. But Darsh was also right. Should the intention matter if we have the right facts? This is a story that the campus deserves to know. That's it. Who brought this story to us is immaterial!" protested Yousuf.

At the back of his mind, he was wondering whether Anil Da would do justice to the half-fry double side he ordered some time ago. While ordering, he spent a good seven minutes, Abhik clocked, explaining the recipe to Anil Da.

"Intention matters, Yousuf. I think it matters. What if Darsh and his poltu Gods are forging the evidence? Who knows they would have bribed these five students with some stupid promises?"

"C'mon, these five students are final years, not second- or third-years, who would get settled with a Maggi. They are here only for a few months. What would you bribe them with? Front row on the star night in SF? Or a bottle of RS from Bhondu?" replied Yousuf with irritation, partially directed at Abhik, and partially at Anil Da, who was delaying his order.

"Fine. But don't you wonder why they went against Jena? After all, Jena was helping them with their placements?"

The irritated Yousuf turned into a smiling Buddha. "Elementary, my dear Abhik! Because despite his best efforts, Jena couldn't get them shortlisted in any of the interviews. Now it's another matter altogether that those five are not day-zero, day-one, or even day-ten candidates. They are six-pointers. And we are only on day five of our placement."

"My Chief-editor-turned-Sherlock, thank you for your investigative journalism! But we need to talk to students from other halls to see whether they have faced any discrimination at the hands of Jena. And finally, we also need to reach out to Jena. Remember, Ada's comment!"

"Of course, by all means. I am not asking us to skip our research. If anything, we should double down. All I am saying is the fact that Darsh brought this story to us shouldn't matter to us."

"Hmm," sighed Abhik. A half-nod.

Rajat followed with another sigh. At the sight of his half-fry double side. The texture and the colour of the dish didn't give him enough confidence to try it. Anil Da stood there, grinning behind his dense moustache, waiting for valuable feedback for the gourmet dish. He even thought to name it YDF – Yousuf Double Fry, if the creator of the dish approved it today.

Yousuf picked the fork and ran it on the white of the egg, carving out a small bite. The yellow, disturbed by the fork, broke into a thick stream like a volcanic eruption. He dipped the bite clung on the head of his fork in the yellow stream. Then in a swift action, the bite travelled from the plate to his mouth, his teeth getting into action. Not bad, his tongue conveyed the message to his brain. Few more tries and it could be perfected, he thought. His respect for Patel hall went up.

Yousuf gave Anil Da, a thumbs-up. "A little more practice Anil Da, and it will be perfect."

The joy of being admired amidst the daily complaints was enough to bring moistness to Anil Da's eyes. He scurried to the door of his kitchen.

"I will try another one right now, and this will be on me," Anil Da shouted without looking back for Yousuf's approval.

"You and your half-fry double side," smiled Abhik at bewildered Yousuf, who was still staring at the door of the kitchen.

The next bite, clinging on Yousuf's fork, was in the air. The bite fell off and splashed in the yellow stream, bringing Yousuf's attention back to Abhik.

Yousuf picked the bite. "You and your Patel hall. Why is everyone here in so much tempo? Anyway, listen, there is something that I wished to speak to you…Umm…What was it?"

He shut and squeezed his eyes. "Yes, about Rajat. Look, the way he charged at Darsh, I felt…"

He stopped midway, at the sight of Halwai approaching them. Abhik turned back to see what made Yousuf stop.

Halwai patted on Abhik's back.

"Great work guys, the first edition rocks! Awaaz is onto something revolutionary, I can see. By the way, who's your next target?"

His probing eyes were fixed on Abhik, ignoring Yousuf's presence.

"The poltu of KGP," said Yousuf, running a blunt knife slowly on the freshly delivered half-fry double side.

Anil Da had looked hard for that knife in his cutlery. After all, it was for Yousuf. It was another matter that Yousuf had never used a knife for eating.

Halwai was forced to look at Yousuf, who didn't bother to look up from his plate. Abhik marvelled at Yousuf's gumption.

"By all means. It does deserve a full-page story. And I will be the first one to share all the insider's stories. So, whenever you are ready," smirked Halwai.

A junior hurling a jibe at a senior was something IIT KGP had yet to accept. Or for that matter, at any college in the world. However, if one thing Halwai had learnt on his journey to a poltu God, it was to swallow your pride if you had to get your work done. And he had to get his work done from Abhik and Yousuf. From Awaaz.

"By the way, have you seen the latest viral video? Displacement?" Halwai quizzed them, his smirk giving way to a condescending smile.

"I heard about it, but..." Abhik tried to answer before he was interrupted by Halwai.

"It's a fantastic piece of work, created by some third-years, Baba and Daroga. You must feature it in your next edition." Halwai patted Abhik's back again. "Bye guys, I have to build my CV. It's a bloody job!"

Both Abhik and Yousuf watched Halwai waddling away. They wondered why Halwai didn't order anything at the canteen. Did he come only to meet them, trying to glean some information from them? They didn't, however, wonder why Halwai was building his CV now. Or maybe they chose to ignore it.

Abhik turned to Yousuf. "Hey, you were saying something about Rajat."

"Yes."

CHAPTER FOUR

KGPians spent their four years in a vain pursuit of *Purushartha*, the object of human life.

In their first year, the aim was to erase the haunting memories of Irodov with the pleasures of standing under the PMT. The attempts to achieve the first goal, *Kama*, were made in classes, in labs, at dance or dramatics societies, and anywhere which allowed the opposite sexes to come together. By the time one came to know that this goal could be achieved by anyone except the freshers, it was too late.

The second year was when they dedicated themselves to the pursuit of the second goal, *Dharma* - their duties towards their own halls, and conduct before other halls. The illusion of walking on a righteous path was soon shattered by the dip in the CGPA at the end of the second year.

With a pragmatic outlook, they entered into their third year, trying to gather means of life or *Arth*, the third goal. Repairing their CGPA, pleasing the professors who could fail them, collecting bullet points that could be added to their CVs, writing others' names on the *khata* at the canteens or stationery shops, and begging, borrowing, and stealing undergarments to class notes – were some of the hunter-gatherer activities they indulged in to lead a meaningful life.

An urge for liberation, or *Moksha*, however, overwhelmed them as soon as they entered into their fourth year, and final year for the lucky ones. The pursuit of their final goal. CGPA was a *maya* – became their tenet. Everyone got a job in the end, even if it's Infosys – became their belief. These souls, aspiring for liberation, preached the concept of *Purushartha* to everyone, especially the freshers, preparing them for the next four years.

And the cycle continued!

Displacement captured the essence of this cycle, especially the last stage of *Moksha*.

A short film that had been downloaded enough on DC++, the peer-to-peer file-sharing platform on the campus, to be declared viral!

The creators of the film, virtually non-existent until now, were basking in new-found glory. Encouraged to further pursue film-making on the campus, Baba and Daroga waited for a creative idea to dawn upon them. And dawn it did. In fact, it came directly from the Gods.

Baba and Daroga were sitting in a room in Patel hall, their borrowed Sony camcorder lying beside them.

The thin-framed Baba was compensated by the chubby Daroga. A duo that aspired to be the Coen brothers but resembled Abbas-Mustan.

The swirls of incense mingled with the wisps of cigarette smoke produced a hallucinating effect in the room. The computer was playing the film – Displacement. Halwai, Chimney, and Darsh were engrossed, even though they had seen it a couple of times.

Daroga had received a call last night from Darsh. Without revealing too much, Darsh promised a creative idea which could be the next project for the duo.

From 14 DTW Waale

The big, bold letters, followed by a photo of 14 youthful faces, announced the end of the film. Baba and Daroga could easily be spotted in the photo, jostling for their few square inches in the crowd of 14.

The viewers of the film turned towards its creators. The suspense around the creative idea was about to be lifted.

"What an exquisite display of craft! So beautifully conceptualised and executed that I can literally feel the passion that drove both of you."

Halwai had rehearsed the choicest compliments to pander to the budding artists. The only thing an artist is hungry for is appreciation for her art, he had read somewhere.

"It's only you who can turn our idea into a reality. No one else" added Chimney to the pandering. "That shot in your movie, where the protagonist, the *ghasi*, who couldn't get a job till the end, was reeling under a swarm of emotions. Walking lonely on the 2.2, staring into the darkness. The camera angle, the music in the background. Mind-blowing. I told

Halwai, that's it. This is our man. Isn't it Halwai? Didn't I say that?"

Chimney turned to Halwai, who had a blankness drawn over his face. Halwai himself was a *ghasi*, a student of Agriculture and Food Engineering department, who couldn't land a job so far.

Chimney tried to break Halwai's reverie. "Isn't it Halwai?"

A forced smile spread across Halwai's face. He nodded softly.

"But what's the idea?" asked Daroga with a restlessness in his voice. Baba nodded.

Halwai mysteriously smiled. "You have been dealing with fictional stories so far. What if we offer you a real story to cover?" He paused to ensure that he had caught the attention of the artists in the room. "A real story of a real person, which you present in your unique style. A real person who is like one of us but who rose to become a leader. Dedicated to the service of IIT KGP."

"Do you mean a documentary?" asked Baba.

"Sort of. But not something which puts people to sleep. Rather one which inspires people. In fact, don't think like a documentary. Think of some new format."

"Yes, we can have new ways to shoot a docu..." Baba attempted to sound like a pro but couldn't complete it.

"One minute, Baba," interrupted Daroga. "Who is the person? And what exactly are we talking about here?"

Daroga is a tough nut to crack, Halwai made a mental note.

He decided to be straightforward. "We are talking about building an image for Darsh for the upcoming VP elections."

A moment of silence followed to absorb what Halwai just said. Baba and Daroga stole a glance at each other before fixing their gaze on Darsh, who had been silent throughout.

Chimney broke the silence. "But it's not at all what you guys are thinking. We are not asking you to build a false image for Darsh. We know your artistic souls will never allow that. The aim here is to prove his worthiness as a VP candidate. Just capture what all he had done in a creative way, package it well, and present it to the junta. See, we ourselves could have done it. But we are not as creative as you are." He chuckled sheepishly.

"We need to think. Besides, I am not sure what can be done creatively," said Daroga, emphasising the last word, looking at Darsh.

He nudged Baba, a signal to leave.

"Can we help you think faster?" asked Halwai, building suspense in the room.

Suddenly, he sprang to the door and latched it at the top. His action confounded those inside the room. Turning back, he riveted his attention on Daroga – the tough nut.

Till last night, he was sure that convincing the filmmakers would be a cakewalk. But now, it didn't seem so. Consequently, his part of the brain – the spontaneous one – which was shaped amidst the rough and tumble of the KGP politics, was lit-up. Working at the speed of light, conjuring up ideas.

As the idea descended upon him, he said calmly, "Darsh, our future VP, has been planning to set up a new society, which would be well funded by the Gymkhana. Do you want to know the name of the society?"

Leaving everyone guessing, Halwai walked up to the window in his room and wrapped his fingers firmly around the green horizontal grills. Staring into the green patch between the C and D wings, often used for football matches, he stayed silent, allowing the idea to acquire a full shape.

Chimney and Darsh, meanwhile, squirmed in their chairs. This was not in the script. They also thought that the makers of Displacement would easily agree with their proposal. If not, a governing position at a suitable existing society would be offered. But a new society!

"Tech Film Society, TFS."

Halwai announced, turning back, and fixing his gaze on his targets.

"And I am sure you are smart enough to guess who Darsh has in mind as the governor of the TFS. Imagine a full-fledged society, with a considerable budget, which will unleash a cinema revolution in the campus. Who knows the next Vishal Bhardwaj will come from our IIT?"

He clapped, excited at the figment of his imagination, paying gratitude to his spontaneous brain. Baba joined him, unable to contain his excitement.

"But…but." Halwai signalled Baba to stop. "This dream will just be a dream if Darsh doesn't win. After all, dreams are the copyright of winners," sighed Halwai. The melancholy in his voice emanated from his past experience.

"We have one condition," said Daroga. The offer on the table seemed to finally crack the tough nut. "We will be given enough freedom. At any point, if we feel we are being dictated, we will have to…" He didn't feel the need to complete his sentence.

"Also, we need to be updated on each and every campaign activity so that we can do our creative job better," added Baba, getting a nod from Daroga.

"Welcome to the team." Halwai raised his hand, his open palm inviting claps from Daroga and Baba. "Now the KGP will witness a campaign never seen before."

The sound of two successive claps echoed within the four walls of the room. Chimney and Darsh smiled, marvelling at the brain that made this moment possible. Darsh could visualise beyond this moment as well.

"But what kind of image do you want to build for Darsh?" asked Baba.

Halwai smiled, ready to answer.

***

"You and down-to-earth?"

Ada's frame shook with a gleeful chuckle, once again puncturing a silent night, once again distracting Darsh.

Jnan Ghosh stadium, named after the first Director of the IIT KGP and situated almost at the centre of the 2.2 circle, hosted Inter-Hall and inter-IIT athletic events, sometimes live shows during SF. This was, however, in the daytime. As the night cloaked the campus, the stadium hosted romantic couples, offering them a space for their serene athletics.

Darsh came straight to meet Ada after his meeting with Baba and Daroga. Amidst the preparations for the end-semester exam, search for an internship, hunting for sponsors for SF, and devising for his election campaign; he was finding it challenging to spend time with her. She knew and hence, hardly ever insisted on a meeting. But today she did. It has been almost a week since they met, and that too briefly, on his birthday.

"C'mon, we are hardly getting any time to meet. And when we meet, you are all excited to pull my leg," complained Darsh, feigning anger, swivelling his face away from her.

"Sorry, sorry…"

She got up and walked to his other side, now facing him. She was fully participating in this cute game of sulking and cajoling. The commotion drew the attention of other couples, for whom the silence the space offered was precious.

She slapped his face gently. "What I meant to say was why you are building a down-to-earth image for yourself. You are what you are!"

"In politics, we are not what we are, my dear!" He returned the slap with the same gentleness. "We have to build an image. And by the way, I am not far away from being down-to-earth."

"Don't get me laughing again. I know it must be your Halwai's idea! The poltu God!"

She enacted a deity showering blessing on her devotees, bringing a smile to his face.

"Your Oscar-worthy acting reminds me what's happening at your Banjara? Any upcoming play where I can see you in your full theatrical glory?"

"Yes, going great. We are rehearsing for a new play. But it could have been better with you by my side."

She winked at him.

"I know. I miss theatre! I wish I could have joined the Banjara after the auditions!"

She knew he had an interest in theatre. That's how they met in the first place! But she always felt his interest to be superficial. Otherwise, he wouldn't have replaced an artistic pursuit with a mundane life at Gymkhana! She resisted in the beginning but, later on, came to terms with his choice, especially after her harrowing experience when she realised the need for good people like him in the Gymkhana.

"Isn't that Sheetal?" He suddenly pointed to a moving silhouette, breaking her chain of thoughts.

"Sorry!" she exclaimed.

"Isn't that Sheetal? Your *happi*?" he repeated. The female hall president became *Happi* in the local lingo. The male hall president, *happa.*

She didn't take much effort to recognise the dark figure. The darkness, she thought, had always been integral to that figure. She winced, not unnoticed by him. He gently put his arms around her, softly squeezing and then rubbing her upper arm.

"It's a past now, Ada. Forget and forgive," he whispered.

"Forget? Forgive?" she shivered. "How can you say that? You know what she did. She could have made my life easier, and my pain subside. But no...As a fellow girl, I had no expectations. Because I had heard this, and it may be true that a woman is a woman's worst enemy! But as a fellow human? All she had to do was…"

She felt a rise of fury within, choking her up. Blurry-eyed, she felt that the dark figure, standing still, was staring at her.

He squeezed her tighter. *It was foolish to bring up the topic of Sheetal. Ada would need more time,* he thought.

He consoled her. "Hey, I didn't mean to hurt you. Let it go. And listen, I have an idea to spend more time together."

"You mean more time to pull your leg!" She was back to her normal.

"Yes, if that's what your goal is. But this has to be secret."

"Okay, you have my attention. Now, no more suspense, please."

"During winter break, I will be going to Bangalore to meet a few sponsors for SF. Why don't you join me? We will chill out in the tech city for a few days, and then you can leave for Kolhapur."

"Not a bad idea. I will not get much time at home though. And I will have to obviously inform you at home about my Bangalore adventure. Not everyone, but one person, for sure. But why secret?"

"Well, if this is out, the first question I will be asked in my election campaign will be what the hell I was doing with my girlfriend when I was supposed to raise sponsorship for SF."

"Hmm…so, I will have something to blackmail you. Then I am completely in for it." Her eyes twinkled, catching the light coming from a floodlight tower.

"You have to decide. Are you going to campaign for me or blackmail me? You can't do both."

"I can. When you are down-to-earth, I will support you. But when you are up-in-sky, I will blackmail you."

Both cracked up. Their laughter confused the romancing couples. *Are the two here to share some private moments or just to laugh?* They can easily do that anywhere on the campus.

He got up. "To win against you is almost impossible. Shall we leave now?"

"You are forgetting something?"

"Ohh, yes."

Leaning forward, he planted a peck on her forehead. The warmth of the peck seeped through her closed eyes. A moment she cherished for as long as she remembered. The first time he kissed her was when he was comforting her in her moments of grief.

***

There were two types of students at IIT KGP. One who would not miss a class they could afford to attend. Others wouldn't attend a class they could afford to miss. Both coexisted on the campus symbiotically.

There were a few classes where both types were seen together. Computer Software was one of them. Not because of the content of the course but because of its professor.

Pawan Kumar, the enigmatic and beloved professor, taught at the Department of Mathematics. If simplicity incarnated itself in a resident of the campus, it would have been professor Pawan Kumar. His thin-framed body walked with the gait of a monk, lost in his thought experiments. Walking was something he truly loved; he had no vehicle, not even a bicycle. Always seen in the same pair of shirt and trousers, he would enter his class in slippers. The dark circles below his eyes would reveal the sleepless nights he probably spent solving mathematical problems that would change the course of humanity. Probably the Goldbach's Conjecture or the Reimann's Hypothesis.

He had attempted JEE twice, ranking two in his first attempt. Not satisfied, he attempted again. Unfortunately, he again ended up with a rank of two!

Raman Auditorium was almost full of students. While other professors were strict about the attendance in their classes, professor Pawan didn't bother at all. *I can't take attendance in such a big class; I would rather spend my ten minutes clarifying the doubts of my students*, he would say.

Sitting on his haunches, the professor was slapping the duster furiously on the ground. Some of the rising chalk dust settled on his bald head.

He was soon back on the board.

"Students, as I said earlier, the resolution principle can't help you with the selection." He pulled out a pink chalk from his shirt pocket and scratched a big cross mark next to where it was written 'Resolution Principle.'

Darsh yawned louder than usual. Not because he felt bored. Because he didn't sleep much last night, after meeting Ada, he went to the Gymkhana to attend the SF core team meeting. With SF hardly a month away, sponsorship was the main focus. Afterwards, Darsh headed back to meet Halwai and Chimney. They had to decide who would shadow Darsh during the election campaigns. Not always following the candidate, the shadow was actually supposed to *become* the candidate when the latter was unavailable. A look-alike was what would qualify for a shadow!

The loud yawn made the heads turn to him. Abhik and Saad, sitting next to him, smiled. Ada, sitting three rows away, pitied him. *She should not insist on late-night meetings*, she thought.

It was the only class common to the four of them. Darsh and Ada knew each other from their first year; their friendship blossomed into love in the second year. That was also when Darsh and Abhik met each other; both were allotted neighbouring rooms in Patel hall. The trio then spotted Saad in Pawan Kumar's class. More than Saad, it was his notes the trio fell in love with!

Feeling embarrassed, Darsh decided to save his losing grace.

He stood up at his place. Amidst the sniggers. "Sir! Can you please explain the term Nolan written above the formula of x square…?"

The sniggers turned into a hearty laugh, to his confusion. Abhik vigorously tugged at his T-shirt, almost pulling him down into his seat.

"That's the name of the author of a book that the Prof has recommended," whispered Abhik to Darsh.

Pursing his mouth in a smirk, Darsh crashed against his seat.

"Students, silence, please!" The professor tried to regain the attention of the class. "If someone is trying to wake up, he should be given an opportunity."

Darsh started pressing the keys of his mobile phone furiously. He looked up after hitting the 'send' key. Ada's phone beeped; the message was delivered.

Turning to Abhik, Darsh whispered, "Look, Abhik, I don't think I can keep my eyes open even for a minute. Let's go to Nescafe."

"But what about the class? We have mid-sem coming up," protested Abhik.

"Let's go, man! Saad is there. We will take his notes."

Saad overheard the conversation. *Not this time, man*, he told himself.

***

The Nescafe next to the Tagore Open Amphitheatre, or TOAT, was not a common place for the students to hang around. Usually, they land here in breaks between two classes or after bunking their classes.

"Can you please explain the term Nolan…?"

Ada mimicked Darsh but broke into laughter before she could finish her act. Abhik gulped down the last sip of iced tea so that he could join Ada. Saad chuckled.

"Okay, guys. Enough. I know I was sleeping. Thanks for reminding me." Darsh sounded annoyed.

Ada took pity on Darsh. Her love for him took over her desire to tease him further.

She tried to divert the conversation. "Saad, we will need your notes the big time. Prof Pawan Kumar is still going over my head."

Saad recalled the promise he made to himself a few hours ago. But he jittered when Ada's eyes continued to linger on him.

She didn't take her eyes off Saad. "You will share. Right?"

"Yes, of course." Saad could only mumble as if in a trance. *He could break all his promises for Ada.*

"Thank God. We are saved. By the way, what's the plan for the winter break? What are you guys doing?" She turned to Abhik.

"Abhik?"

"Well, I am visiting Saad's place for a few days, his village in Bihar. And then I will be off to my place."

Ada looked at Saad, making him nervous again. "That's cool! Saad, you never invited us."

She turned to Darsh. "And Darsh, what's your plan?" A suppressed smile on her lips went unnoticed by others.

"I have to be in Bangalore to meet a few sponsors for SF. So, yes. I will be in the lap of the tech city. And if there is some time left, I will visit my uncle in Mumbai."

"So, no home this time?" asked Abhik.

"Nope. Not this time."

What Darsh didn't share was the fact that he had gone home only once in the last two and a half years.

Abhik looked at Ada. "And what about you, Ada?"

"I will go straight home. Unlike you guys, we don't have the freedom to roam around, go to our friends' places or sit in the lap of cities," sighed Ada.

"Look, who's saying! A girl from Kolhapur who came all the way to IIT KGP, skipping IIT Bombay. No freedom. Bullshit!" jumped in Darsh. He didn't want to leave the opportunity to return her tease.

Ada didn't react, she was lost in her dreams. Walking on the streets of Bangalore with Darsh.

As all of them rose to leave, Darsh went closer to Abhik and placed his hands on Abhik's shoulders.

"Thank you, man!"

Darsh's expression of gratitude triggered a quizzical look on Abhik's face.

"For publishing that article against Jena. I am glad that he is kicked out of the Place Com. He was ruining it," clarified Darsh.

"Ohh! That. No need to say thanks. I was just doing my job. Sorry, it took some time for us to investigate and analyse the evidence. But doing the right thing always takes time. Hope you understand."

Darsh dug his fingers deeper into Abhik's shoulders. "That's completely understood. But I am glad you did the right thing."

"Yes, the right thing. We always have to do the right thing," nodded Abhik thoughtfully.

CHAPTER FIVE

The ordinary red building of Kharagpur railway station didn't give any hint of the fact that it was home to India's longest train platform or that many extraordinary minds had been to that platform. Comfortable in its obscurity, the building seems to be frozen in the passage of time. Redolent of the era it lived in.

Saad and Abhik were standing in a queue for tickets, constantly looking at the digital noticeboard displaying the train schedule. They were on their way to Howrah station, from where they had a connecting train to Buxar.

Saad threw a tense look at a casually standing Abhik.

"We have to hurry Abhik. If we miss this train to Howrah, we will not be able to catch the Vibhuti Express. And then the next train is tomorrow morning. We will have to spend the night at Howrah station."

"Will that not be cool?" smiled Abhik, with mischief in his eyes. "We can roam around in *Amar Sonar Bangla* Walk on the Howrah bridge, visit Belur Math, go to Sonagachi, and..."

"Hello, we are going to my village. Not Kolkata. And I hope you know what Sonagachi is. It's not really a tree of gold, as the name suggests. It's a tree to climb somewhere else."

Saad winked at Abhik. Abhik smiled, not at the joke but at the sight of a taciturn Saad opening up.

"Stop lying, you labour class!"

A roaring voice boomed. All eyes turned to the source of the commotion. Two shaking figures were at the scene.

One from anger and another from fear.

The ticket checker was panting badly, his pot belly expanding and contracting in rhythm with his shallow breaths.

The person at the receiving end was middle-aged, covered in a tattered vest and a *dhoti*.

A crowd slowly started gathering around them.

Abhik's feet rose in the direction of the crowd. Saad tried to stop him. "Abhik, we have to catch the train!"

"Don't worry, I will be back in a minute. You get the tickets."

Abhik sprang towards the scene.

Tearing through the crowd, Abhik now stood a few inches away from the *perpetrator* and the *victim* as he labelled them in his mind.

"First of all, you travel in an express train with a local train ticket," shouted the ticket checker at the top of his lungs, his eyes occasionally meeting the eyes of the crowd. "And then you are blatantly lying that you have travelled in a local train. Show me which local train has come from Howrah in the last two hours." He pointed to the digital display.

The *victim* stood folding his hands in front of the perpetrator, shivering like the tatters on his body would in a gust of wind.

The silence from the other side riled the ticket checker. He boomed again. "Show me now. Else, come to jail with me if you can't pay the fine."

The ticket checker clasped the shivering arm of the person, muttering under his breath. "You labour class people have…"

"Wait, Dada. Let him speak first," intervened Abhik. He gently placed his hands on the ticket checker's arms, a signal for the latter to loosen his clasp. "And why are you addressing him as a labour class? Have you forgotten where you are standing? The land of hammer and sickle."

Stunned, the ticket checker didn't expect anything like this to come from the crowd. After all, they were supposed to be onlookers. And precisely for the same reason, the shivering person didn't expect it either. But at least his shiver came to a halt.

The person, emboldened by Abhik's presence, opened up. "Dada, I swear to *Maa Kaali*. I travelled by a local train from Howrah." He picked up a crumpled piece of paper from the floor and flattened it out. "And here is my ticket. You can see the date and time on it."

He handed it over to Abhik as if Abhik would give the final verdict.

The ticket checker, as if in a last bid to regain control, raised his voice as much as he could. "I know that's a valid ticket, but you have travelled by an express train. Not a local train. You are lying. There is no local train that has come in the last two hours."

"I came much earlier. I have been waiting at the platform," replied the person, looking at Abhik.

"That's a lie. I saw you getting down from the express train that had just arrived. And not from any ordinary coach. But from the AC coach."

"I just wanted to see what an AC coach looks like," mumbled the person, lowering his eyes as if ashamed of his act. Abhik, however, heard it clearly.

The ticket checker made an intimidating move towards the person. "What…what did you say?"

"Dada, let him go. You have no right to hold him up. He has a valid ticket. That's all," declared Abhik. He patted the shoulder of the person. "You go now and take care of yourself!"

"Hey, hey…who are you to pass a judgement? I am the ticket checker here. Just because you are from IIT doesn't mean you know everything. Let me do my job."

The ticket checker was furious, his demeanour expressing his deep-seated disgust at IITians. How they flock from all over the country to Kharagpur, only to take away and never to give back!

"Go ahead then. Do your job. I will file an RTI against you. Then you will have to answer why you fined this man. And if your answer is not found satisfactory, then only God can save you," said Abhik with a certain carelessness.

The murmurs among the crowd rose. The enigmatic word – RTI – had its impact. The pleasure-seeking casual onlookers wore the seriousness of responsible citizens. They waited for the ticket checker to respond.

"What…what is RTI?" asked the ticket checker nervously.

"You don't know RTI. Are you serious? You are a government officer, and you don't know RTI. You should be jailed for your ignorance."

The ticket checker by now was struggling to speak, beads of sweat appearing on his forehead. "Listen, I know you are making all this up. There is nothing like RTI. But…but I am, out of my own judgement and compassion…I am…I will leave this person. But only this time."

Abhik smiled. He felt a tug at his shirt. Saad was standing there. He whispered to Abhik. "Abhik let's go. The train is almost here."

"Thank you, Dada, for your kind judgement and compassion. But…"

Abhik couldn't finish as Saad started pulling him by his arm. Abhik started drifting along with Saad. The crowd parted in a hurry, making way for both of them, especially for the one who saved the victim from the perpetrator.

Abhik looked back and shouted, "Dada, RTI is for real. I am not making it up. Look for yourself!"

He could see Dada's face, confusion and anger written all over. He could see two folded hands rising up, a display of gratitude to the saviour.

Moving away from the crowd, as Saad and Abhik were about to enter the subway, they heard the announcement. Their train had arrived at the platform.

"Let's run Saad. Our train is here. Why are we walking?" asked Abhik innocently.

"Thank you for reminding me. Had it not been for your act of bravado…"

"Oh, man! Let's run. You can thank me later." Abhik dashed into the subway.

"Hey, Abhik," shouted Saad while running after Abhik. "What was that RTI thing?"

"Nothing. I was trying to scare the ticket checker. I mean, the RTI is for real. It was passed two years ago. But God knows, what will be its fate?"

***

"Why do you always have to do the right thing?"

Saad raised his voice over the din of the *jhaalmuri* hawker parading in the coach. Abhik was sitting right across from him. The window seat on the local train to Howrah offered an immersive view of the countryside.

"Dada," Abhik called the *jhaalmuri* hawker, who appeared in no time.

"Two *jhaalmuri,*" ordered Abhik.

The hawker put the paraphernalia, hanging from his neck, down on the floor. A big tin container surrounded by smaller steel containers at its circumference. From the top, it appeared like the cylinder of a pistol loaded with bullets. Every small container contained one ingredient for the *jhaalmuri* – diced boiled potatoes, roasted peanuts, spices or *moshla*, long pieces of fresh coconut, and finely chopped tomatoes, onion, green chillies, ginger, cucumber, and coriander. A green plastic bottle stuck out of one of these containers. The big container had *muri* or puffed rice inside it, covered with a lid. Next to the lid was a heap of lemons and tomatoes. The hawker opened the lid, scooped out a generous dose of puffed rice, and put it in an empty container. In a swift, choreographed action, he scooped out every ingredient one after the other and placed them in the container. The bullets were fired in succession. The constant clatter of metal striking against one another added the perfect music to the choreography. The green bottle was snapped out of its place and squeezed into the container. A jet of liquid hit the heap inside the container. The air was laden with a prickly aroma of mustard oil.

"Dada, green chillies are fine?" asked the hawker while stirring the container.

Conscious that his station had almost arrived, he sped up the stirring. Receiving no answer, he repeated his question, a little louder this time.

"Yes, yes…absolutely, Dada. Without chillies, how will *jhaalmuri* become *jhaal*?" smiled Abhik, inviting stares from other commuters. For them, it was the *moshla*, not the chillies, which made the *jhaalmuri jhaal*.

The hawker sprinkled chopped chillies over the *jhaalmuri*, gave another stirring, and heaped the final blend in two paper cones. A long piece of fresh coconut was inserted in each cone – the final act of garnishing the *jhaalmuri*.

The train came to a halt. The hawker hurriedly handed over the cones to Abhik, lifted his paraphernalia, and hung it from his neck. As soon as he collected the money from Abhik, he dashed for the coach's door. He had to almost jump off the running train.

"Now you got your answer," said Abhik, passing one cone to Saad, who returned a quizzical look.

"That hawker," continued Abhik, taking a bite off the coconut piece, "could have easily saved a few seconds by not repeating his question about chillies, and would have gone ahead stuffing them, making our dish super *jhaal*. But he asked us again. Do you know why? Because he wanted to do the right thing."

Saad clearly seemed unimpressed. "He was just doing his work; he was paid for it," he said.

"We are also paid," chuckled Abhik. "Our studies at this prestigious institute of the country are paid by millions of taxpayers. So, if they are paying us, should we not work for them or do the right thing, as I say?"

"That logic is…I don't completely buy into it."

"You may or may not. But that's the truth. Now, your real question is *why*. Why do I or we need to do the right things? Right?"

Saad sighed, still not convinced by Abhik's logic. But he trusted him.

"Because if we don't do the right things, trust is broken. And they will do the wrong things?" said Abhik, looking outside the window. The train had caught speed, and so had Abhik's thoughts.

"Who, they?" asked Saad. No response came from Abhik.

"Who, they?" repeated Saad, this time in a raised voice.

"There are many *them*, Saad. My father was one of *them*."

A soft groan escaped Abhik. He continued staring outside the window at the passing denuded trees, which waited eagerly for spring.

Saad could see a teardrop pushed out from the corner of Abhik's eye by the wind, making a trail to Abhik's ear.

Abhik suddenly turned to Saad and the other passengers. "I don't think it's the chillies that make *jhaalmuri jhaal*. But it's *moshla*," he said, with a big grin on his face.

The trail of teardrop was getting dried up by the same wind.

***

The Cafe Coffee Day at Brigade Road was abuzz with constant chatter and clatter. The whirr of the coffee machine, the incessant movement of the barista, the frequent swivel of the glass doors, the impatient fingers punching the laptop keys, the upbeat conversations punctuated by sips of coffee.

The excitement was palpable in the air, offering a glimpse into the future of the city that was Bangalore.

"*Deva re deva*! It's so expensive!" exclaimed Ada, her one hand holding the menu card and the other pressed against her bosom. She flipped the menu card. "Let me look for the cheapest item on the menu."

Her finger kept sliding down the menu card until it found its destination. With a smile of victory, she started looking for a barista. Darsh was unusually silent all this while.

"Madam, that is an add-on. You will have to order a coffee along with that." The barista humbly suggested, when Ada ordered for cocoa topping from the menu.

"What?"

She let out an incredulous gasp. She took a few moments to gather herself. "What if I only need the add-on? No coffee."

She stared intently into the eyes of the barista, who started jittering.

"Bring two Cappuccinos please," intervened Darsh, sparing the barista from her wrath. The barista hurriedly left.

"Hey, why did you intervene?" she said, slightly irritated. "I could have easily managed the situation."

"And why did you intervene? I could also have easily managed the situation," he huffed.

Ada understood the reference. It was about the meeting they had this morning at the Airtel office. Darsh was pitching for sponsorship for the Spring Festival.

"I was just helping you, Darsh. I saw you fumbling when the marketing head asked you about the rough gender break-up. It was a simple question, I know. You could have easily answered, I have no doubt. But…I saw you fumbling…"

"But it was my damn meeting. You were only supposed to be a listener." He raised his voice slightly.

"But nobody will ever know I was there. The marketing head is not going to tell anyone," she said, in a matter-of-factly tone.

He kept silent, his nostrils flaring.

"What? Is it your male ego that is hurt? A girl was helping you…"

"That's bullshit! You know that."

"Glad to hear that! Then what is it?"

"It's just that…when I take up something, it's my baby. I have to take it to the finish line!"

"Why are you so obsessed with *I*? Last year, when I was in trouble, you came to support me. Did I say then it's my matter, stay away?"

"That was a different matter. You can't compare the two!"

"Why not? What happened today at the sponsor's meeting was exactly the same. One of us was in trouble. Another came to help."

"I was not in trouble. You were in trouble. And I had saved you," he blurted, raising his finger at her.

She was stunned into silence for a moment.

"So, it is your male ego," she said, without taking her eyes off him, who had lowered his by now.

A silence followed, only to be broken by the barista, who was ready to serve the coffee.

"Madam, Sir, your hot Cappuccino. Enjoy!"

The barista smiled at them. Ada returned the smile. Fearing she might again charge upon him, the barista scurried away. She started sipping her coffee, bringing her attention back to Darsh. He was still looking down. A good two minutes passed before anyone spoke.

He finally mustered the courage to speak.

"I am sorry, Ada. I shouldn't have said that," he said in a regretful tone. "But you know that it has nothing to do with my male ego. That's not who I am."

She gently placed her fingers on Darsh's hand. I know Darsh. And that's why I want to keep reminding you. The Darsh, whom I adored, with whom I have fallen in love with, I don't want him to change even a bit."

He smiled, his eyes meeting hers. He pressed his lips against each other, nodding his head gently.

"Yes, I want you to be the Darsh who saved a girl when she was in trouble. But do not think of it as a favour you are doing to her. Rather, it's just the right thing you are doing. Like you did when you stopped the rehearsal when a slipper was hurled at you."

"Wait! What! You still remember that?" he asked in an astonished tone.

"Remember? Are you kidding? That's what made me fall in love with you," she said, bringing a faint blush to his cheeks. "We were ready for our final rehearsal before the final show. And it was supposed to be a hooting rehearsal, preparing us for the great adulation showered by the audience." She slowly started drifting into an actor's zone.

"Yes, nobody came to see a drama put together by freshers. They only came to hoot, which is a bigger drama for them. What a pity!" He shook his head.

"But kudos to our HTDS governors; they cared so much for us that they felt that we should be prepared for the onslaught," she said, clapping gently. HTDS stood for Hindi Technology Dramatics Society. "And then they brought the hooters. I guess they were the governors of ETDS."

"Yes, they were. How can I forget them? All of them looked like hunters on the prowl. Honestly, I wouldn't have reacted the way I did had Arunabh stopped after throwing the first slipper?"

"What then made you revolt? The second slipper?" she asked. Although she knew the answer, after all, she was a spectator of the incident; hearing it directly from him had its own joy.

"First of all, I was badly tired of the day-long rehearsals. My character had so many mouthful dialogues. Remembering them was a bloody nightmare. I still don't know what that play, Jalta Hua Rath, was about. Now, at this so-called hooting rehearsal..." The foyer of the main building flashed before his eyes, the entire cast of the play standing nervously before the hooters. “I kept my calm for long after the hooters started interrupting us, shouting at us. When the first slipper came flying, and even though I understood it was not meant to harm us physically, I was shocked for a moment. I gathered myself and continued. But somewhere, I also made up my mind that I would not stay silent if it happened again. After all, why the hell were we doing this play? To take slippers. Being a senior doesn’t mean you can do anything. What about our dignity? And then all hell broke loose when the second slipper landed. I had to simply stop and walk away from the stage. There was no other option.”

“I know. Standing in the corner of the stage, playing my almost no-dialogue role, I had a similar thought. And I remember the look on Arunabh’s face. A senior insulted by his junior,” she remarked, a victorious smile spreading on her face. As if her victory was contained in his.

“Thank God, you were not given any dialogues. Otherwise, that play would have been doomed from day one.”

“Shut up! Those amateur governors would never have recognised my acting prowess. I am glad that I finally found my home in Banjara.”

“Well...that is probably the only thing where I would completely agree with you.”

“Then, why don’t you come and join us?” she appealed, with genuine affection in her voice.

"Who said I have left drama? Poltu has more drama in it than the real drama," he smiled.

"Shut up again! You and your poltu!"

"But do you know this?" he said, suddenly excited. "After that incident, when I was cycling back to my hall, all of a sudden, Arunabh appeared next to me. I was a little scared; after all, I was a fresher, and he was two years older than me. He kept on cycling for a while and then said, I will take you out for dinner sometime."

She jumped out of her seat. "Wow! You never told me this. How was the dinner with him?"

"He never took me out."

Both bust out laughing.

"Anyway, that reminds me, what's our dinner plan? Because soon after that I have to catch the bus for Kolhapur," she asked, looking at her watch.

***

The gurgle of the canal was musical to the ears. The rising sun on a misty horizon was soothing to the eyes. The fragrance of the fresh milk was pleasant to the nostrils. The winter breeze was freezing cold to the skin. The taste of the *babool* twig was sweet to the tongue.

All senses are immersed and awake.

Saad and Abhik, clad from top to bottom in woollens, were sitting on a bamboo bridge over the canal, brushing their teeth with *babool* twigs, dangling their feet. Occasionally, a breeze would make them shiver, and the bamboo bridge would rattle. Two glasses of fresh milk lay next to them, ready to be gulped as soon as the twigs had done their cleansing act.

They were in Saad's village – Anwarhi, a nondescript village in Rohtas district. After the train ferried them from Howrah to Buxar, they took a rickety and jam-packed bus to Gunsej, a journey of almost an hour. Thankfully, the bright coldness of winter prevented the bus from turning into a sweat-producing cauldron. At some point, after marvelling at the travellers on the roof of the bus, Abhik got tempted to become one of them. Saad tried his best to desist Abhik from exhibiting his bravado. But as soon as the bus stopped to pick up passengers, Abhik rushed to the back of the bus, clambered up the ladder, and made his way to the roof amidst the crowd. At the Gunsej bus stand, when the bus stopped, and both of them met again, Abhik simply smiled at Saad, whose frowns were still intact. A journey on foot of another seven kilometres alongside a canal, a part of the Sone canal system, finally brought them to their destination.

"Can you imagine this canal was constructed by the British in the 1860s?" a shivering Saad said. "Sone river and its canals turned this whole region into an island of prosperity. My father used to tell me how the canal was used to transport rice, wheat, grains, and other stuff. All of that has gone now. The canal also doesn't get its share of the water supply. The farmers have dug up borewells. Something needs to be done. Otherwise, this area will turn dry and barren." He lamented while sipping from his glass of milk.

"Something *right* needs to be done," quipped Abhik.

"Yes, Mr. Right," responded Saad sarcastically. "You know what your epitaph will say? How wrong is it to bury Mr Right here?"

Both of them cackled with laughter.

"Can I ask you something?" asked Saad hesitatingly. Abhik nodded in the affirmative.

"What is it about your father? You mentioned something on the train. But then you...."

Saad's voice quivered. Whether it was the chilly wind or the question itself that made him quiver, he was not sure.

Abhik stopped sipping his milk. His eyes wandered to the water beneath his feet, which surprisingly was still. As if to allow him to clearly see himself and search for the answer.

"If you don't feel like sharing, it's alright," said Saad.

"He was a Naxalite," replied Abhik.

The moment he uttered these words, the still water trembled slightly. The water seemed to be mimicking his mind.

He turned to Saad. "I have never really shared this with anyone. We come from a place called Jangalpur. It's in Rajnandgaon district in Chhattisgarh. I don't have too many memories about it. I was there only till the age of eight. But it was pretty much like your village. A small, sleepy village in the lap of nature. What my mother always told me is that she was kept in the dark; she never knew that my father was a Naxalite. It was only after their marriage that she came to know. She was devastated. I have faint memories of armed people coming to our home late at night and leaving before the crack of dawn. All they spoke about was pain, problems, and injustice. All they carried were rifles, or maybe just sticks, long sticks, I am not sure. Anyway, one day, my father disappeared. My mother waited for a few days, but he didn't return. We left for Raipur, to my *mama*'s home. I have been raised there."

"Did he come back?" asked Saad.

"No. Not yet. But we are not waiting anymore." Abhik was again staring at the water, which was flowing now.

"And you think something wrong was done to your..."

"I don't know," interrupted Abhik. "I don't know what circumstances forced him to take up arms. But after reading all these stories about Naxalites and the history of Naxalism, I think we have not done the right things for them. We broke their trust. And hence, they have gone the wrong way."

"I was asking about your mother," said Saad, who had patiently waited Abhik to finish.

Their eyes met, and silence followed.

Saad broke the silence. "Don't you think your mother had suffered more than your father? Her trust was broken. Yet, she didn't do the wrong thing. Rather, she raised you and made sure that you went to IIT. I know you have a philosophy of right and wrong. And you apply the philosophy everywhere, to everyone. But what I believe is that there is right or wrong - *only in the moment*. If I believe it's right at this moment, I will do it. But if I find the same thing wrong at some other moment, I will not do it. See, context matters."

"That's called convenience, my friend. Not context" protested Abhik.

"Okay, answer this. You know Newton's model and quantum theory. Right?"

"Yes, of course. Thanks to HC Verma. My physics was impeccable."

"So, you also know that Newton's model is valid only for large objects but fails in the atomic world, where quantum theory takes over. Now, that doesn't mean that Newton's model is wrong, or quantum theory is right. Both have their own places. In their own context."

"Hmm…" escaped Abhik. But he soon retorted, "No, no. That's still convenience."

"Well, you may be right. But I am also right. At least at this moment," said Saad with a smile.

Abhik couldn't help but smile. "As long as you keep supplying your notes, you are right."

Abhik winked at Saad, who didn't react. Saad's face wore a grim silence.

Abhik patted Saad's back. "What happened? Okay, fine. Next time, I will make sure your notes are not painted with fish curry!"

"Sometimes I think you, Darsh and Ada are with me only for my notes. I don't really fit among you. Look at all of you. Darsh is contesting for VP elections; you are the editor of Awaaz, and Ada is into dramatics. And look at me. I am just a notes-guy," said Saad in a grim voice.

"Hey, come on! That's not right. I don't know about others. But I certainly enjoy your company. Well, we might have met you because of your notes. See, finally, all of us met others because of something. Darsh and I bonded over *sutta*. He liked a certain brand, which I liked too," chuckled Abhik. "How he and Ada met. Well, that's a long story! But it's not because of *sutta* or notes that we continue our friendship."

Abhik again patted Saad's back, this time a little harder.

"What's the story of Ada and Darsh?" asked Saad, a serious expression blanketing his face.

"That's a long story, Saad. I am not fully aware. They met through the Dramatics Society in the first year. That's all I know."

"Do you think they are meant for each other?' Saad looked at Abhik, who gave a curious look in return. "I mean, look at Darsh, all pomp-and-show Delhi *wallah*. And Ada, a simple girl from Kolhapur. Simple people need to be with simple people."

"Like you?" blurted Abhik.

"Sorry? Wha…what are you trying to say?" Saad was caught off guard.

"Look, Saad. I know that you have feelings for Ada. But you also know that she and…"

"Yes, yes. I know all of that." It was as if Saad didn't want to hear the rest of it. "And I don't really have emotions for her. It's just that I like her."

It was Saad's turn to look at the reflections in the water and search for answers.

***

The Mahalakshmi temple, or *Ambabai Mandir,* was one of the *Shakti Peethas,* the seat of the Shakti, the Goddess of power. The city of Kolhapur revolved around this temple, which was supposed to be 1800 years old. The five *shikharas* in conical shape, painted in pale lime colour, stood in deep contrast to the dark grey stone of the temple. On a bright sunny day, it evoked an image of a static golden-yellow flame in a dark grey crucible. The courtyard, spacious and naturally lit, had many small temples, along with *deepstambh*, tall lamp stands. The outer circumference of the courtyard was lined with shops, which catered to the needs of the devotees.

In one of the shops, an old man clad in a white *kurta* and *pyjama* and a cap, a traditional attire of Maharashtra, was reading his morning newspaper. His face wore the weariness of a seventy-year-old man who had raised five girls and a boy: his only means being his shop in the temple courtyard and a small *pedha* factory. His eyes, however, reflected a deep sense of satisfaction - of raising them well and of living a well-meaning life. His shop was a one-stop destination for the devotees, who never failed to notice the two framed photos hanging on the wall. One of them showed the man, in his prime, greeting Atal Bihari Vajpayee, and the other greeting Indira Gandhi. The two iconic Prime ministers of India.

The man, like most of us, had found his calling at some point but couldn't follow it, like most of us.

A woman, draped in a traditional Maharashtrian *saree*, slightly bent at her waist, was approaching the shop with a limping gait. One end of her *saree* was pulled down to cover her face, a departure from how women in Maharashtra usually dressed.

The woman stuttered in a husky voice. "Five incense sticks, a matchstick, one vermillion casket, a photo of *Ambabai,* and half *pedha*."

The old man looked up from his newspaper. After examining the woman, he said, "Why don't you take the complete plate of worship? It has everything that you want and more. Here, look at it." The man forwarded the plate.

"No, just give me what I want," replied the woman rudely.

The man was upset but continued, "Fine. But I don't give half *pedha*. You will have to take at least a hundred grams."

The woman's tone got sharper. "My *Ambabai* wants only half *pedha*. Who are you to decide? Give me what I want."

"Sorry, I can't. You can go to another shop," said the man firmly and went back to his newspaper.

"What Hanumant Chavan? You have such a big shop, and you can't give half *pedha*."

Shocked, the man looked closely at the woman. It's not usual even for those who knew him to address him by his name. He was addressed as *Dada*.

The woman, in a swift action, pulled up the loose end of her *saree* to reveal her face.

Hanumant almost jumped off his chair. "You, little brat. You are playing with me."

He rushed out of the shop and hugged the *woman*, ignoring the surreptitious looks of the passers-by.

"When did you come, and what is this all drama, Ada?" he asked in a complaining tone.

"Dada, how could you not know? Who asks for half *pedha*?" Ada almost collapsed in convulsions, which made her *saree* unwrap, revealing her normal attire beneath.

"One who is *yeda*, a total mad!" quipped Hanumant and joined Ada's laughter. "Let's have our favourite *misal*. Gotya, take care of the shop." He shouted at his helper.

Ambling out of the temple courtyard, the grandfather and the granddaughter didn't look like two people separated by generations, but two souls connected by trust. Their relationship was defined not by one instructing another but rather by one believing in another. Ada had spent almost five years of her childhood at her Dada's home in Kolhapur when her parents were struggling to make ends meet. The memories that Ada carried to this day were that of her walking with Dada to his small pedha factory and watching the mixture of *khoya*, milk, sugar, and flavouring spices simmering over a stove. When the mixture started to pull away from the sides of the hot pan, that's when it achieved the desired thickness; Dada used to show her. But all the eight-year-old Ada cared about was when the *pedha* would be ready to be gobbled up!

Just outside the entrance of the temple, they headed to their favourite *missal* shop - Gaikwad Misal. A rusty board dangling at the entrance of the shop welcomed them. Ada observed that the board hadn't changed a bit since her childhood. A bright orange Marathi pheta (turban), two folded hands, and Marathi text - *Jevalya Ya. Come to eat.*

They occupied their usual bench in a corner from where Ada could see one of the *shikhars* of the temple from a small window at the top. That window had been her childhood fascination.

"Gaikwad, two *missal*, extra spicy. Totally *zanzanit*!" Hanumant waved at the owner of the shop, who reciprocated with a grinning smile.

"Dada, I will not have it too spicy!" said Ada.

"What? A *Marathi mulgi* is saying no to spicy. Are you alright? What has IIT Kharagpur done to you?"

His remark evoked a smile on her face, which was soon replaced by furrows on her forehead.

"What is it?" he asked.

"Dada, you know Darsh?"

He replied. "Yes, the one who helped you last year with…You were in Bangalore with him. Right?" She nodded. He continued, "What about him? You were in love with him? Right?" He stated, as a matter of fact.

She frowned, "Ssshhh…Dada, how can you ask such questions so loud in public?"

He came back with a pat reply, "Only you can play pranks on me in public."

She winced. He realised that she was really distressed.

"Sorry, go ahead. Tell me what about him," he asked.

"You know how he stood by me throughout that incident. Never left me, even for a single moment. I saw in him a kind, empathetic, and considerate Darsh. And that's what brought me closer to him. But now I see glimpses of his other side. One who is ego-driven wants to dominate and cares less for others. I don't know whether I am reading too much. Maybe he is also stressed by the campaigns."

"Campaigns?"

"Yes, he is contesting for the post of the Vice President."

"Politics!" He heaved a sigh.

The hot *missal* with *paav* arrived in steel plates, each with three pockets. The biggest pocket was overflowing with the *missal,* garnished with salty snacks or *farsaan.* Hot red. A specially prepared Maharashtrian spice, *goda masala*, lent the *missal* its real spiciness. *Zanzanit.* The second pocket had *paav,* the ubiquitous bun, and the third cut pieces of lemon and onion.

"We all have both sides, Ada," continued Hanumant. "We are born as virtuous but slowly acquire the sins of the world. Some of us lose the balance between the good and bad, the right and wrong.

That's where things go wrong. Ask Darsh to retain his balance. Politics can diminish his ability to see clearly, to judge right from wrong, to retain the balance," he said, chewing his missal-soaked pav. He muttered under his breath, "Like, I almost lost mine!"

"But Dada, does that mean that one keeps on doing wrong things as long as the balance is maintained?" she retorted. She waved at the waiter for water; the *missal* was getting unbearable.

"Well, the real question is how do you perceive right and wrong? Maintaining balance then comes naturally to you," he said.

"What do you mean by *perceive*? There is something called right and something wrong. Why perceive?"

"It's not that easy Ada. Let's talk about your incident. The one you faced, where Darsh helped you. You shared it with me. But you haven't shared the same with anyone else in your family, including your parents, who have done so much for you. Is that right or wrong?"

She opened up after a moment of silence, "What I did was right. They would never have understood. Worse, they could have pulled me out of college. You know how adamant they were that I only went to IIT Bombay. Why? Because it's close to our home. It didn't matter to them at all what department I was getting there. Metallurgy. And look, here I am in the electrical department; the prospects are so much better.

Thanks to you, Dada, for fighting with them. I was ready to give up."

"So, you feel you were right. But your parents, once they come to know, will be devastated. You will be wrong in their eyes. But to me, you are just walking the path of balance. Once you understand this balance, my child, your life will be easier," he said, his eyes gauging her state of mind. She gave a confused look. "Don't worry! The realisation will dawn on its own. How are your other gang members? Abhik and Sadhu?"

She cracked up, "It's not Sadhu. It's Saad. But yes, he is like a *sadhu*, a total monk. I like him a lot."

He smiled.

"Dada, you were also into politics at some point. What happened?" she asked as if she was suddenly reminded.

"That's a story for some other time, dear. Now, focus on your *missal*."

CHAPTER SIX

Everyone at IIT KGP waited eagerly for the spring. After a cold spell of placements and mid-semester exams, the students looked forward to being reinvigorated by the hope that the spring promised. Humans hope for what they don't have or what they can't achieve easily. Same was true at IIT KGP. Those who couldn't get a job offer at the campus placements hoped for an off-campus placement. Those who scored low on mid-semester exams hoped to improve their score in the end-semester exams. Those who never won any Gymkhana elections hoped to win this time. And those who never dated a girl, thanks to the skewed gender ratio on the campus, hoped to find one at the Spring Festival.

Spring Fest was what really brought spring to the campus. As new leaves unfurled on trees, welcoming birds to perch, IIT KGP would welcome a swarm of carefree souls from all across the country for a three-day celebration, arguably the largest in Asia. The decibel level would shoot through the roof, the eateries would buzz day and night, the love birds would jostle for the cosy corners, booze would stream uninterrupted, and the nerds would retreat further in their shells. The campus would be plastered with posters of the musicians and bands gracing the Star

Nite at the TOAT, Tagore Open Air Theatre. This year, it was an Indian rock back – Indian Ocean, and a singing sensation from Bollywood - Shaan and Kailash Kher. The arena, the hub for major activities during the fest, would host a multitude of events, turning into a battlefield, encompassing various genres like Dance, Music, Dramatics, Photography, Literature, Quizzing, and Fine Arts. Some of these events, like Nukkad (dramatics), Shuffle (dance) and Wildfire (western music), would conduct their preliminary rounds nationwide. The prize money was handsome, thanks to the sponsors who believed in 'The True Spirit of Youth,' as the slogan of the fest went.

The Bhatnagar auditorium was waiting to receive the contestants for its next event, Mime. Ada, the head of Nukkad, was sitting alone in the auditorium, going through the registration list. The sub-heads were yet to report to her. The jury was yet to arrive. After coming back from Kolhapur, she had been trying to decipher what Dada told her about maintaining balance. After all, she wanted to see Darsh in the *right* way. *The real question is how do you perceive right and wrong*. Dada's words rang clearly in her ears. What was not clear was the bloody word - perceive. *What is right is right, what is wrong is wrong*, Ada shouted in her head. *Then, what is it about perceiving? She* continued debating inside. She would have gone on had she not been interrupted by a voice from the door.

"Is the registration still open?"

The face behind the voice startled her. It was Sheetal.

With an inscrutable face, Ada said, "Yes, you can register."

Sheetal walked up to Ada and started writing her name on a piece of paper. She could hear Ada's heartbeat. Suddenly, she stopped writing and looked at Ada. "Ada, I know that I was at fault, but I had no option."

Sheetal had been mustering the courage to speak to Ada. Guilt festered within her for a long.

"If you have registered, you can take a seat or come back after some time," said Ada, tersely, without looking at Sheetal.

"Listen, Ada." Sheetal sounded impatient, her heartbeat now matching Ada's. "I could have stood for you; I could have become a witness. But that professor…when I bumped into you after that incident…"

"That chapter is over." Ada almost shrieked. "You did what you felt was right. But if you had…" She abruptly stopped. The import of what she just said hit her. *You did what you felt was right.* How could she say that? *What is right is right, what is wrong is wrong.* Her head started pounding.

"Is this the venue for Mime?"

A bunch of giggling faces appeared at the door. Ada felt like shouting at them, too. But all she could do was nod. Sheetal started walking up the aisle to take a seat. In no time, the auditorium was bustling with contestants. Many of them, who were theatrically trained, had their faces painted in white, lips in red, and eyes and brows outlined with black. Ada felt like hiding behind a similar mask, which only revealed what she wished to show, not what was going on inside her. The jury arrived. Ada had asked her sub-heads, two second-years, to lead the event. She was not sure if she would be able to sit throughout the event.

One of the sub-heads took the stage and invited the first team - Patna Women's College. A group of girls appeared. All were clad in white, stoles of different colours tied around their waists, and faces painted. One of them, who looked like the leader of the group, bowed down to the stage while climbing up the stage - a ritual to show reverence for the space. Someone shouted from the back, 'Yo Vatsala!' On the stage, they organised themselves in a formation that resembled a cradle lulling a baby to sleep. As the performance unfolded, depicting the travails of a girl from birth to youth, the audience gasped. Ada felt she couldn't hold it any longer. She walked out quietly, her body shivering.

***

The Perpz area, an all-day dance floor, was throbbing with the frenetic energy of the gyrating bodies. On the stage was the host, a girl brimming with energy, who was exhorting everyone to keep tapping their feet. *Let the energy flow; let the music play!* Hollering constantly into a cordless mike, she was on the verge of rupturing her jugular vein. The DJ was trying hard to keep pace with incoming requests for songs. In between, some dancing feet were leaping onto the stage from the floor, accompanying the host for some time and then jumping back on the floor. The rickety stage was protesting at every such leap.

In a corner, Ada stood. Not sure how she landed here when all she was looking for was loneliness. How could her mind equate this madness to serenity? She couldn't fathom. But now, her mind would not let her move. The heady cocktail of audio and visual spellbound her. One part of her wanted to jump into the madness, merging into the pulsating crowd and losing her identity. And another part wished to stand silently, looking inside, and affirming her identity. *Which part was right, which was wrong? Or was it all perspective?* She shut her eyes and plugged her ears. A silence gushed inside her; she felt at peace. *This has to be right.* A few moments passed by. She felt the noise creeping up her body, finding a way inside her, displacing the silence. *This was wrong.* A few more moments passed by. She felt silent; she felt noisy. She felt *both*. She felt right, she felt wrong. She felt *both. Or did she just feel balanced?*

She opened her eyes. Everything was hazy - the dancing crowd, the stage, the girl on the stage, her mike, the DJ, the stalls in the back, the big hoardings with the sponsors' logos, the institute buildings, the trees, the sky. Everything seemed to be contained in a big bubble, expanding yet static, full of randomly moving particles colliding with each other. She, herself, was a big cloud of particles.

She saw Darsh in the crowd - a misty figure of dancing particles, some were brightly lit, some were dark - happily moving in the big bubble. *Why did he stand up for her?* The bright particles became brighter. *Will he go to any extent to win the elections?* The dark particles became darker.

She started looking for others.

Abhik, Saad, Amrita, Security Didi, Supercop Jha, Pawan Kumar, Dada…

She looked harder, looked closer.

That's when she decided to lift herself off the ground and hover in the air. She could do it effortlessly. Now she could see all of them.

A bunch of particles. Nothing more. Nothing less.

***

The roof of the Gymkhana was hosting a boisterous celebration tonight. It had almost been a week since the Spring Festival ended. The residual din had dissipated. The festival teams, fatigued but upbeat, had gathered at their usual *adda* to rejoice at their success. The Gymkhana, officially called Technology Students' Gymkhana, was an impressive spread-out building which controlled the numerous extra-curricular and co-curricular activities at IIT KGP. The building overlooked a lake, which surrounded a small island - a wilderness of weeds, bushes, and a few trees. At night, the lit-up building of the Gymkhana cast its reflection in the serene waters, creating an impression of a drifting building.

Like the many drifting dreams and aspirations that it housed.

Divakar, the current General Secretary, Social and Cultural, was admiring the reflection. His own aspiration of climbing up the political ladder was nurtured under this roof. Only to be drifted later. Partially because of the succumbing pressure of his parents, who got freaked out at his poor academic performance. After all, it was a cardinal sin to score a CGPA below seven under the watch of Bengali parents. While he was a strong contender for the position of VP, he humbly backed out. Much to the chagrin of the poltu Gods of his hall. Much to the delight of Darsh and Mahe.

Divakar turned his attention to the boisterous crowd.

"My countrymen," he addressed them. He had a flair for language. When he was admitted to the BC Roy hospital on account of chicken pox, as the legend goes, the only book he carried with him was *Word Power Made Easy*. "Finally, we have done it. The biggest SF in the history of the KGP!" He raised his hand, inviting uninterrupted applause from the audience.

"A footfall of more than 35000, more than 300 colleges, a total cash prize worth around 20 Lakhs, and a total budget of 55 Lakhs. We are probably the biggest college fest in all of Asia."

The audience roared. They knew it was big but never imagined it to be this big!

"And we could become the biggest because we have the best team here. Look at the feedback from Shaan. He was extremely pleased with his reception at the airport, accommodation on the campus, and the arrangements at his performance. Indian Ocean said they were yet to see a better college than ours. And Kailash Kher. He has left a sweet note in his husky, soothing voice for all of us. The media is all gaga about the fest. Frankly, I feel we had flawless operations."

The audience cheered again, self-congratulating their performance.

"But the credit also goes to those who brought moolah."

Divakar waited for his last word to sink in. After seeing a few confused faces, he gestured with his fingers. Smiles erupted on the confused faces.

"All those who raised sponsorship, a big salute to all of them," continued Divakar, "Especially to Darsh, who single-handedly raised 15 Lakhs from Airtel in Bangalore."

Divakar looked at Darsh, raising his clapping hands. Shouts of *Yo Darsh* sprouted. Darsh acknowledged the cheers with a broad smile. A few in the audience grimaced as they knew the politics behind this recognition.

"And now is the time for celebration. The Cal party!" Divakar threw both his hands in the air.

The audience, especially the second-years, sprang in the air. As the tradition went, every year, after the successful conclusion of the Spring Festival, the organisers held the celebrations in Calcutta. A day full of fun and frolic in the City of Joy! Clearly, the profit made out of the festival sponsored the party.

As soon as the date of the party was decided, the crowd started dispersing. Darsh went up to Divakar and hugged him.

"Thank you, Divakar! For trusting me with the Airtel deal!" said Darsh in a tone filled with gratitude.

"No worries, my friend," said Divakar. "Any day. I am sure this deal will help you in the elections. I can go to any extent to keep that Mahe out of the VP race. I just hate him. You are more deserving. Although, a little less than me." He chuckled. Darsh responded with a smile.

CHAPTER SEVEN

The foyer of Vikramshila was draped in yellow light. The light poles - square columns with globes of yellow light at the top - were surrounding the three editors of Awaaz. The fourth one had dropped out of the guild. Three months after its beginning, Awaaz had become synonymous with responsible journalism - one which wrote about the real issues of the campus fearlessly! The fact that some of the editors from the rival magazine, Scholars' Avenue, had moved to Awaaz was an indication of its growing popularity. Abhik, one day, received a congratulatory email out of the blue from a journalist from Indian Express. How did she come to know about Awaaz? Abhik couldn't really figure it out. What elated him, however, was the fact that it came from Indian Express, which had Rajkamal Jha, his role model, as its Chief Editor.

"Abhik, we don't have much time to think about it! I know it might be a hard decision for you."

Rajat, pacing in front of Abhik and Yousuf, had summoned this emergency meeting as he had access to an *explosive* story.

"And why do you think so?" Abhik hollered at Rajat. "Just because Darsh is involved here."

Rajat didn't react. He wanted Abhik to continue.

"Listen, I have always said this. Friendships will never come in our way of doing the right things. And what I have also said is that our homework should absolutely be top notch. Because once the magazine is out..."

Rajat knew this was the right time to intervene. "I will take responsibility for the homework. I have already done enough research on this. And, if anything, I will double down." Rajat's demeanour oozed a strange confidence, one that seemed to be driven by a feeling of revenge.

"But do we realise that publishing this story just a few weeks before the Gymkhana elections will sound like a cheap publicity stunt?" Yousuf jumped into the conversation.

He had grown suspicious of Rajat's motives. Since the day Rajat attacked Darsh when the latter brought Jena's story, Yousuf has been observing Rajat closely. When Abhik dismissed his idea of approaching the HR department for sponsorship, Rajat turned indifferent to Awaaz. Then, all of a sudden, he became active as if he was coached by someone. And now he had come up with an explosive story. Against Darsh.

Abhik was aware of Yousuf's suspicion. But he dismissed it whenever Yousuf expressed his concern.

Abhik responded, "That is immaterial, Yousuf. We are not here to time our stories. We are here to write. Just write. About what is right."

Rajat smiled. His ploy was working. Sabu would be happy with him.

Yousuf pressed upon his point. "I know Abhik. But listen to me. Why does this story sound to me like nothing more than a publicity stunt? The SF team works their ass off to raise sponsorship. Now, if they are spending a part of the profit on some Cal party, they deserve it. How can it be a story? Since when did splurging money from your own hard-earned money become a crime? Now, if we write about this, we know we will mainly be targeting Darsh, who has raised a handsome sponsorship. And he is contesting for the VP. It will look like we are against him and favouring another candidate. Mahe, or whoever that is. It's a flimsy ground on which we are building our story."

Rajat waited patiently for Yousuf to finish. He had rehearsed this conversation over and over with Sabu. He pulled out his first argument from his loaded quiver.

"Yousuf, you forgot, but we wrote against Jena, who was a potential VP candidate against Darsh. And I know you will say that it's not the same. But let me share my views on why I feel what Darsh, rather the SF committee, had done is a far greater crime than what Jena did."

Yousuf and Abhik silently stared at Rajat, who was standing directly under one of the globes of light. A small puddle of shadow was formed around his feet. The luminous glow of the light from the top couldn't match the gloom of the shadow.

Yousuf continued, "The SF committee raises money from sponsors for the fest. Now, some of it is being spent organising the SF. A part of the leftover profit is spent on a party. Fair enough, they deserve it. But how much do they deserve, and who decides? See, I don't have a problem with spending money on a party. But I have a serious problem with who is keeping track of the money spent. How much of it was actually spent on the party, and how much of it has gone to their pockets? There are no written records, no approvals, nothing. What I have found is that a good part goes to the administration's pocket, and the rest goes to the heads of the SF committee. Now, the heads who are contesting use this money for their election campaigns. This is where Darsh comes into the picture. He raised 15 Lakhs from Airtel. I am sure he must be pocketing something out of this for his campaigning." Rajat stopped, heaving a sigh. He had more arguments in his quiver. But he was sure they wouldn't be needed.

Abhik maintained a stern face.

"But all of this is a conjecture," said Yousuf. He wouldn't relent easily.

"Yes," replied Rajat. "And that's why, allow me to come back with more evidence and testimonies. And if you find the story worthy of publishing, please put it under editorial, signed by Abhik."

"Why Abhik? You can sign it off," protested Yousuf.

"Remember, we had agreed that all the editorials will be signed by Abhik as the Chief Editor. The HMC story, the Jena story, all of them were signed by him," argued Rajat.

There was silence.

"Listen, Abhik, I know I am putting you in a tough spot," continued Rajat, turning to Abhik, who was in a pensive mood, looking down. This would probably be the last argument from Rajat's quiver. "But this has to be done. After the Jena story, many fingers have been raised on us, on our integrity. We are seen on Darsh's side. I want to correct it. I don't want us to be seen as biased. More importantly, I don't want to see your dream of creating something so beautiful crashing down. I believe in you!"

He waited for Abhik's reaction. Slowly lifting his eyes, Abhik nodded.

"Thank you, Abhik, for believing in me. Give me a week's time. I will come back to both of you."

Rajat headed to the bicycle stand. He was on a mission to make his hall proud. Curling his fingers around his bicycle's handles, he muttered under his breath, *Chutiya.*

Yousuf looked at Abhik, who was wearing a pensive look. He put his hands on Abhik's shoulder. "You don't have to do this, Abhik. Besides, I smell something fishy. The way Rajat had attacked Darsh last time, the way he is now pushing this story. Who knows his intentions? After all, he is from the same hall as Mahe."

Abhik looked up and asked, "So, you believe that intentions matter."

"Yes, of course, they do. Otherwise..." Yousuf suddenly stopped. Something crossed his mind. *Should the intention matter if we have the right facts?*

Abhik smiled, "Who brought the story to us is immaterial. We will go ahead."

***

It had been a week since the three editors met at Vikramshila. Rajat had come back with substantial evidence and presented it to Abhik and Yousuf. Abhik finally gave approval to the story. Yousuf had no choice but to agree. Abhik asked Rajat to interview the SF committee members, especially Darsh, and include their comments in the story - a practice they followed religiously after their first story. Rajat promptly agreed to it. He offered the story to be signed by him so as to ease Abhik's situation. Abhik thanked him for his gesture but decided to stick to his responsibility as the Chief Editor. When the final story was ready, they went through it a million times - scrutinising every word, questioning every allegation, interpreting every comment, and debating the conclusion. They knew the repercussions the story would have. It would rile the SF committee, upset the administration, and change the course of the election. While they extensively mulled over these topics, what they couldn't fathom was that it would probably cost a friendship!

A day before the magazine with the explosive story hit the stands, Abhik was feeling restless. His inner turmoil was cracking his armour of righteousness. Sitting alone in his room, he started flickering through the book - *If You Are Afraid Of Heights*. The first page had a short biography of Rajkamal Jha, the author. It read - Rajkamal Jha is a mechanical engineering graduate from the Indian Institute of Technology and has a master's degree in journalism from the University of Southern California, Los Angeles... Abhik had started exploring courses in journalism. A couple of pages later, he saw the quote from another book - Mr. Vertigo, authored by Paul Auster. Even though he had read the quote so many times that he remembered every word of it, every time, he felt like reading it afresh.

Deep down, I don't believe it takes any special talent for a person to lift himself off the ground and hover in the air. We all have it in us - every man, woman, and child... You must learn to stop being yourself. That's where it begins, and everything else follows from that.

His rumination was interrupted by a beep on Gtalk. Did he see a message from Ada - *Wazz up? Long time!* He stared at the message for some time and then replied - *Can we meet? I have an explosive story to share!*

***

"Hey, what was that message on Gtalk? Some explosive story?" asked Ada.

After the exchange of the messages, within an hour, Ada and Abhik met at the gate of the Gymkhana. And now they were strolling on the 2.2.

"Well, I can't tell you the story. It's explosive for sure!" he answered, smiling at her curiosity.

He suddenly realised that he had not met or spoken to her after her SF episode. What he heard was that she got dizzy in the Perpz area, fell down, and was brought to her hall. He got all these updates from Saad, who managed to meet her once.

"Hey, sorry, I should have asked about your well-being first. How are you now? After that SF episode? I feel bad I didn't call you or meet you," he sounded regretful.

"Another treat then, Mr. Abhik! You now owe me two treats," she laughed, bringing a smile back to his face. "Well, I am good now. I didn't share that experience with anyone except my Dada." She stopped abruptly; something crossed her mind.

"Go ahead, I am listening," he said after waiting for a few moments.

She looked at him. With a sigh, she asked, "Can we sit?"

They sat on the pavement of the road.

She began, "I am glad that I fell down that day. Otherwise, it was becoming too heavy for me. It's only when I felt I could lift myself up. I could see everyone. I saw Darsh, I saw you, I saw Saad, I saw everyone while hovering in the air, not like how I saw you guys every day. But I saw who you *really* were. I can't explain. And you know it's so easy to lift yourself up; it doesn't need much effort." She again stopped to catch a glimpse of him.

He was silent, stunned by listening to her experience and its uncanny resemblance to what he read today.

"I know it will not make sense. It didn't to me either. It was only when I spoke to Dada that I could make some sense of this mess. Anyway, let's talk about something normal. What's that explosive story!"

"Yours is more explosive!" He came out of his silence.

She gleefully remarked, "But you can't publish this in Awaaz."

"That's true!" he said, "I don't know what to tell you, Ada. And I also don't know why I am telling you. It may be because you pinged me. It may be because I had to listen to your experience and make meaning out of it for myself. It may be something else."

She didn't respond; she just kept looking at him, giving him time to open up.

"I know that this story, this explosive story, will change everything. But I also know it's the right thing to do. It may be wrong for those...who are involved, who are accused. A part of me, a really small part, is pulling me back from publishing this story. Probably, I am not able to lift myself up like you had." He dug his face into his open palms.

"It's alright, Abhik." She placed her hands gently on his head. "No need to be so stressed. If you feel you are right, just go ahead. What will follow will follow. We don't have control over that."

"Whatever follows, promise me that we will be friends. I can't lose another one," he said in a dejected voice, looking away from her.

She got an idea of what it was all about. She scanned the 2.2, from one end to another, bathed in the streetlight. She felt that it was dissolving into a cloud of particles.

"You have my promise," she replied as if in a trance.

CHAPTER EIGHT

After spring came the election season in KGP. For the next month, the campus would turn into a battleground. The poltu Gods would draw strategies for the campaigns, especially targeting the freshers - the first-time voters. While the pact system was long dead, the optimistic Gods still tried to forge strategic alliances. They would set up an army of aides to keep an eye on the activities of the rivals. The candidates in the run would get a complete makeover. Paeans of praise would be written for them. They would be projected as saviours of the campus. If Spring Festival turned the campus into a newborn, the election festival would prepare the newborn for the real world!

Hall Day offered a perfect occasion for campaigning. No one really knew how the tradition of the Hall Day started. Probably one day, some genius realised that while boys could easily visit other boys' rooms, girls were deprived of this opportunity. And that genius, for sure, was a boy. So, he came up with the idea of Hall Day - a day of fun and celebration - when anyone can visit anyone's room. Eventually, the idea stuck around, and every hall started celebrating Hall Days. Over time, another genius, who must be a poltu God or a candidate, came up with the idea of using Hall Days for campaigning. This idea gave a strong reason for the Hall

Days to continue. Since then, all the candidates running for Secretaries, General Secretaries, and Vice President would flock to the Hall Days to woo the voters.

"The first cut is excellent, Baba and Daroga. The down-to-earth image is almost there. Let's get it ready by our Hall Day. We will make it larger-than-life. When the crowd is there, we will switch off all the lights. And boom! We will project this movie on the screen. No one has ever attempted such a thing before!"

Halwai was jumping, excited at his own idea.

Baba and Daroga had finally come up with the first cut of a movie, which they believed was somewhere between a fiction and a documentary. It chronicled Darsh's journey, starting from his achievements - right from getting an A in Engineering Drawing in his first year to raising 15 Lakhs for the fest - and ending with his promises as the future VP. Humility was imprinted all over the Darsh's character. A character that was fictional and real!

Halwai's room, where the movie was just screened, was houseful. It was slowly turning into a war room for the VP's election. Chimney, as usual, was busy seeing the smoke spiralling up. Apart from Darsh, Baba, and Daroga, there were two new faces - Gullu, who was supposed to shadow Darsh in the campaign, and Tunda, who was supposed to ensure that the rivals were afraid of their own shadows!

"Thank you, everyone," said Daroga humbly. "We will further work on it. It will be ready by Hall Day.

And Darsh, we need to sit with you again. Need some more information." He looked at Darsh.

"There is one scene, I think, we should…delete. I never did that," said Darsh hesitatingly. Quizzical eyes turned to him. "I never coached Gullu in swimming. It was the other way around. He is a far better swimmer than I am. And everyone knows that. He won a gold medal in Inter IIT. I have won nothing."

"Hey, hey…you don't need to really become down-to-earth," chuckled Halwai. "You know who gave this idea?"

He pointed to Gullu. Darsh threw a surprised look at Gullu.

"Anything for the hall!" Gullu returned the surprise with a smile.

Darsh heaved a sigh, and then, all of a sudden, he hugged Gullu.

"Now that we are done with all that brotherly love, let's talk business," announced Halwai. "Gullu, you know what you have to do as a shadow of Darsh."

Gullu gave a straight answer. "Yes, I have to represent him during the campaigns, where he is unable to make it and where people don't know him by face."

"That's right. But please don't say I am Vikramaditya Gulati while introducing yourself to the crowd. I know you are capable of doing that. So, just reminding you. And you, Tunda? What are you supposed to do?"

Tunda was startled. He was ogling at a girl's photo on the computer screen.

Chimney walked up to him, looked at the screen. "Hmm…A second year!" He then tapped on Tunda's head. "Pay attention here first. You will have all the time in the world to ogle!"

Thud. Thud. Thud.

A series of loud knocks drew everyone's attention to the door.

Halwai latched open the door. Hota, another member of the war room, was standing there, huffing. He flapped a bundle of papers in front of Halwai's face. Halwai grabbed the papers. *Awaaz* was written in big and bold on top of it.

"Editorial," puffed out Hota.

Halwai turned the pages till he came across the editorial. His eyes widened, his nostrils flared up, and a nerve protruded on his forehead. *Son of a bitch* is all he could say before he slapped the papers on Darsh's hands.

***

"Your bloody friend! How could he even do that? I know…I know…." said Halwai, pacing furiously in the room. "It's Sabu. He is doing it again. Playing his tricks."

The papers that raised the furore were lying on the floor as if someone molested and slapped them hard on the floor. The editorial headline - The real spring is for the SF committee! - was still visible, and a pair of eyes were silently staring at it, especially at the author's name. The editorial dwelt upon the misuse of the funds raised for the Spring Festival and proposed checks and balances for the future. It insinuated that the senior SF committee members siphoned money off for their personal use. Darsh was mentioned as one of the members!

"How can they explicitly mention the names?" screamed Baba, frustrated.

Darsh suddenly stood up and started stomping on the papers. Halwai rushed to him, held him by his arms, and almost pushed him to the bed.

Halwai started scheming up. "Hold your anger, my friend! Reserve it for another day. We need to prepare a rebuttal."

"I…I have to share something else." Hota stuttered a little. "I know this may not be the right time or right place. But I…I feel it's important." He glanced at Darsh, who was again staring at the papers.

"Go ahead. It better be important," growled Halwai.

"Last evening, I went to Abhik's room. Not to meet him, but his roommate, Guppi. We are in the same department. The room was open; no one was there. I thought to wait for Guppi. So, I started fiddling with the computer. Abhik's Gmail account was open. There was a chat box open. I read the messages. Abhik was asking someone to meet to discuss an explosive story."

"He must be chatting with one of his Awaaz members," intervened Chimney.

"No. It was not any Awaaz member. It was..."

"C'mon, don't be Abbas-Mustan. Speak out the name." Halwai sounded impatient.

"Ada."

Darsh looked up. His expression changed to that of someone who had been stabbed twice!

***

The temperature was soaring in D-324. Darsh was pacing like a maniac, one of his hands clenched into a fist, holding a crushed ball of paper. Abhik was sitting calmly on his chair, his eyes following Darsh. After Hota's revelation, Darsh couldn't hold himself back. He stormed out of the room, rage writ large on his face. Halwai didn't stop him this time.

"You call this crap Awaaz. It's not the voice of KGP. It's Just the voice of a few dumbheads," shouted Darsh, his face twisted with anger.

He aimed the ball at the open window. The ball hit a grill on the window and landed on the floor. Abhik calmly got up from his chair, walked to the ball of paper, and picked it up. Unfolding it, he started straightening the creases.

"You can unwrinkle that, Abhik. But what about the wrinkles you have stamped on my candidature by writing this totally baseless and crappy story," growled

Darsh. He didn't seem to be so concerned about the wrinkles in their friendship.

"What makes you believe it's baseless, Darsh?" retorted Abhik. "We have done the same due diligence as we had for Jena's story. Rajat had collected evidence and testimonies. He tried to verify them as much as possible with different sources. He tried to speak to some of you, but you all declined. Your entire SF committee works opaquely. It's all behind the curtains!"

"But what's the basis behind the allegation that we are pocketing money!"

"It's an allegation. And a well-researched allegation. If there is money left after all the spectacle, where is it going? It's not going into some institute fund, for sure. So, where is it going?"

"Bullshit! What research are you talking about? Some bullshit theories. Let me tell you what. You and your dumbhead Awaaz team are looking for quick and cheap publicity! And what could have been a better target than SF? And linking it with elections."

"I knew that was coming," said Darsh while taking his seat.

"Yes. Because it is the only truth, let me tell you how you came up with this story. You started with two stories. One is on HMC, and the other is on Jena, which I shared with you. They put you in the limelight. And make you feel that you are custodians of truth. Now, what next? You wanted a grander story. But there was none. You saw SF. You were dazzled by its scale. Then you realise elections are also coming up. Why not link the two and concoct a story?"

"Darsh, you can leave now. I don't think we should be continuing with this conversation now. Let's do it later."

"Ha ha ha…" Darsh laughed his guts out. "Do you think there is a later? We are done, Abhik. By the way, no one, and I repeat, no one approached any of the SF members for their comments. Rajat has lied to you. And I will tell you why. He has a motive. He is from RP. The same hall from where my rival is contesting."

"It's not possible," protested Abhik with all his might. "I personally saw him dialling you and others, none of you picked up. He showed me the exchange of messages where you and others declined to comment. I have seen it all with my own eyes."

"Abhik, how can you be so naive? He showed you everything on his phone, and you just believed it. Do you think after knowing that you are going to ruin my prospect, I wouldn't have come to you? Anyway, you have done the *right* thing. I now need to do mine."

Darsh turned towards the door. Abhik's face was deadpan.

"By the way." Darsh turned back to look at Abhik. One last time. "Revealing such investigative stories to others before they get published is not ethical journalism."

"What do you mean? Only three of us knew about this story. We didn't even share it with our other team members." Abhik glared at Darsh.

"You better know what I mean." Darsh slammed the door.

A gust of wind rushed through the window, blowing the pages of Abhik's favourite book. The quote by Paul Auster was staring at him.

***

Abhik was cycling like a madman on the 2.2, his destination being RP Hall. Darsh's comment was playing like a broken record in his head. *He showed you everything on his phone, and you just believed it.* After Darsh left, he frantically tried calling Rajat, but there was no response.

Entering the RP Hall, a part of Abhik was screaming that Darsh was right. He wanted to shoot that part down. And the only way to do that, he realised, was to constantly remind himself why he trusted Rajat in the first place. Rajat was the first one to join Awaaz when it was all just an idea. In those late-night meetings they did, Rajat never left them midway. Even when, on one occasion, he had a test the next day! He was the one who negotiated with the printer in Gole Bazaar to bring the price down to 35 rupees per copy. He brought such good talent to the team. The graphic designer, Vikas, who created the Panji Dude - a cartoon character that became iconic on the campus, was so amazing. Always working in the backdrop, he never asked for the limelight. Always throwing new ideas, even after receiving frequent rejections. He was no less than the founder of Awaaz; how could he possibly think of destroying it?

Abhik didn't realise that he was standing outside Rajat's room. He stopped shy of pushing the door open when he heard hysterical laughter coming from behind.

A bulky voice was congratulating someone. "Great work, Rajat! You finally did it. I must say that I was a little sceptical. But how precisely and neatly you have executed our plan."

What followed was Rajat's unmistakable voice. "Thank you, Sabu, for your faith in me. It was not so easy to convince those two *chutiye*. It took so many rounds of discussions!"

"How did you do that?"

"I worked hard on getting the evidence, some of it real, some fake. It was slightly easy to get the numbers - how much they raised; how much was spent. Rancho, our SF member, helped me a lot. But it was impossible to prove that they were pocketing money. Now, that had to be a part of the story. So, I took a risk. I showed Abhik that I was trying my best to get comments from Darsh and others, but no one was responding. I showed him messages that Darsh had declined. I tried calling Darsh in front of Abhik. I argued that they were hiding something if they were declining to comment. It took time, but Abhik bought into this argument."

"And how did you manage to get those messages from Darsh and others?" asked a different voice.

"It was easy, Mahe," answered Rajat, "I saved Rancho's number by the name of Darsh."

"And what if Abhik would have called Darsh directly from his phone." Mahe again questioned.

"I would have been thrown out of Awaaz. But who the hell, anyway, wished to continue there?" The anguish in Rajat's voice didn't go unnoticed by Abhik, who had his ears still pressed to the door. "I gave so much to Awaaz. But hardly any acknowledgement. All the limelight went to Abhik and Yousuf. I gave so many ideas. But I have no respect for them. Huh…I was, anyway, counting my days at Awaaz!"

Abhik was frozen, his eyes moist. *He was no less than the founder of Awaaz; how could he possibly think of destroying it?* He had his answers. He never made Rajat feel like a founder.

***

Ada was tossing in her bed. It was well past midnight. She had been trying to call Darsh and Abhik throughout the day. But none responded. After reading the story in Awaaz, her mind was racing with an ominous foreboding of a clash between the two. While she sincerely hoped that she was wrong, she was reminded of the *balance* between right and wrong. *Were Darsh and Abhik just balancing each other?*

She thought of giving a call to Saad again. She had called him earlier in the day. He was equally clueless. He promised that he would try to meet Abhik and call her back.

A persistent knock on the door stopped her from making the call. *Who could that be at this time?* She unlatched the door. Amrita was standing there, weeping profusely. When Ada asked her what happened, she hugged Ada tightly.

CHAPTER NINE

"You seem to have no ambition at all, Mr. IITian. I pray Darsh doesn't become a copy of you."

Darsh, engrossed in preparing for the upcoming IIT JEE screening exam, was distracted by his mother's shrieking voice. This was not the first time he had heard his parents fighting. It all started with squabbles when they shifted from Mumbai to Delhi almost two years ago, slowly turning into high-decibel fights. Darsh's father, Rabindra, was working a highly paid job at a multinational company in Mumbai. Darsh, it was clear, would follow in his footsteps. First, IIT, then IIM, and then a lucrative job, most likely in a foreign country. So, he was enrolled on different coaching classes right from grade nine. His mother, though an economist by training, had chosen to be a homemaker and pursue her hobby of classical singing. The small family of three couldn't have asked for a better life. In a turn of events, his father met one of his batchmates, who had quit his corporate career to work for farmers in his native village. Swayed by his passion and argument about how IITians were draining away taxpayers' money by working for these MNCs, Rabindra started pondering over dedicating himself to the service of the nation. *After evaluating a host of ideas, ranging from setting up a dairy farm in his village to joining a political party, he finally settled on shifting to a public sector company in Delhi. He realised that his family would not be able to bear the shock of other ideas. He was wrong. His family couldn't even bear this shock!*

A lower salary, slashed almost by half, would mean a simpler lifestyle. Besides, Delhi was not appealing to the sensibilities of Darsh's mother. She put her best arguments to dissuade him how he could monetarily support the initiatives of his nation-building friends or how he would be better equipped to do all of this after 15 or 20 years when he would have made money. She roped in their family, relatives, friends - everyone she thought could help her bring him to his senses. But nothing worked. In the end, she threatened to leave him. A hollow threat, she also knew. Darsh was a mute spectator to this drama. He was not sure how it would impact him. But in the last two years, every day, he wished he could go back to Mumbai, not for a lavish lifestyle, but for a sane life.

"Stop talking nonsense, Manju. It's nothing to do with my ambition, you know that. It was for the…the…," fumbled Rabindra, looking for the right word.

"The country," hollered Manju. "Say it, come on. You and your country. You are just signing files here and running errands for the ministers. What are you doing for the country?"

Rabindra raised his eyebrows, his eyes meeting Manju's steely glance.

"The truth is you have killed your ambitions," continued Manju, undeterred. "And I don't blame you. That stupid friend of yours, who is sitting idly in his village

in the name of nation-building, is the one to blame. You are not building but depriving the nation of the wealth that you and other IITians could create. The public sector is doomed."

Rabindra had heard this argument multiple times, often backed by reasoning that only an economist could make. But he didn't want to relent so easily. "Why don't you tell your truth? It's you who feel deprived of wealth. Not the nation."

The sharp sting of words was enough to make the corners of Manju's eyes moist. Her youngest sister was getting married. She wanted to gift her a pair of golden bangles. Every time she approached him, asking for money, he discarded her request by citing it as a waste of money.

"Yes, I feel deprived. Your son feels deprived. All of us feel deprived. It's only you, your bloody friends, and your bloody nation which feels wealthy." Manju raised her voice several notches higher.

Darsh tried to plug his ears with his fingers. He knew that the volleys of counterarguments would be endless, each one being delivered on a pitch higher than the previous one. Initially, he was not convinced that his father was unambitious. He thought his father was just naive, easily swayed by someone's sermons. But slowly, he realised that his mother could be right. In the last two years, their lifestyle had degraded. Darsh had to pull out of his coaching classes and mostly prepare on his own. His mother, on many occasions, thought of taking up teaching in a school. But given that these were crucial years for Darsh, she decided to pay her complete attention to home. Despite the dwindling finances, his father never thought of going back to a private job. Worse, he kept on working without asking for any pay raise or promotion for the last two years. It was as if he had found meaning in leaving home at ten in the morning and coming back by five in the evening. To him, this was how the nation was built.

Darsh was staring at a framed photo of his parents, standing on his desk next to his computer. He didn't bring the photo; he never felt the need. He found it nicely tucked within the layers of his clothes in one of his two big bags, which he landed at IIT KGP. Whether it was his mother or father, he was not sure! And he never bothered to find out. That the two-quarrelling people in his life were replaced by their photos was comforting enough for him.

The photo was shot in a studio with a beautiful background, that of snowcapped hills. His mother, adorned in a pink saree, had a radiant smile on her face. Her eyes were staring lovingly into the camera as if trying to peer into their future. His father was carrying a straight face, early sparkles of idealism visible in his eyes. Darsh kept staring intently at the faces, and they started distorting. The father's face morphed into Abhik's. And the mother's into Ada's. The two people he hated the most were replaced by the two he had started hating now.

Darsh jolted himself, shaking the images of Abhik and Ada out of his rumbling head. In a swift action, he plucked the frame and dumped it into the heap of soiled clothes lying on the floor. The half of the frame, carrying the father's photo, was peeping out of the heap.

He made a vow to himself. "I will never be like you. Unambitious. I will not let anyone come between me and my ambitions."

***

Ada was sweating, the beads on her forehead catching the light coming from the window glass. The humid August of Kharagpur was at its worst. She had requested the invigilator to open the windows. But he didn't pay any attention. Why would he when there was no one else in the room!

She was reappearing for an exam that she missed last month owing to her bad health. She had to run around the professor's office, one of the busiest ones in the electrical department, to schedule the exam. At last, the professor assigned the menial task of re-exam to one of his research fellows. Now, she had to run around the research fellow. He not only assumed the responsibility assigned to him but also the authority that was not assigned to him. At KGP, the students who came through the glorified JEE took a dim view of the research fellows, nicknamed rassa. *It's only during such times that the rassa were able to show their superiority!*

So, here was Ada sitting in a room in her department, staring at the exam questions. Invigilated by the research fellow. He was an average-built man with a receding hairline and sunken eyes. Wearing an untucked half-sleeve shirt over a black trouser, he was engrossed in playing the classic game of snake on his mobile, sitting on his invigilator's chair. There was still half an hour to go. Ada requested an additional writing sheet, but it fell on a deaf ear. She raised her voice slightly, but the same result. She stood up and almost shouted at the research fellow. The mobile phone almost fell out of his hands. He looked up, disgruntled. Slowly, he walked up to Ada and slapped the additional sheet on her desk. Least bothered by his rudeness, she just wanted to finish off her exam and walk out of the room.

After a few moments, she felt the weight of a shadow on her. An immobile shadow. She could feel a warm breath pouring down on the nape of her neck. Her fingers loosened their grip on the pen out of shock. The pen started rolling. On the writing sheet, first. Then, on the desk. Reaching the edge of the desk, it stopped. Poised. She felt a rigidity seeping inside her, stopping her from looking back at the shadow. "Run to the door," someone shrieked inside her head. But her frozen limbs didn't cooperate. The shadow was growing on her, the breath becoming heavier. In the next moment, the palm of a hand landed on the side of her neck, slowly slipping inside her T-shirt. The pen rolled off the desk, crashing on the floor. The sound made her body shiver. The next couple of seconds were a complete blur to her. Rub of fingers on her neck as she stood up. Tug at her T-shirt as its collar got entangled in retracting fingers. Screech of the chair as she pushed it back. A flutter of papers as she swiped the writing sheets off the desk. Creak of the door as she flung it open. Before she could dash out of the room completely, she paused for a moment to look back at the shadow.

The invigilator was smiling from the corners of his sunken eyes.

When out of the room, Ada kept on walking briskly until she felt her trembling legs would give up. She realised that she had left her bicycle in the parking lot of her department. The thought of going near the building made her shudder.

"Are you alright? Why are you sweating so much?" She heard a familiar voice.

Sheetal, her senior from her department, was standing in front of her. She didn't know what to answer, she simply broke down. Sheetal grasped something was sorely wrong. She took Ada to the nearby Nescafe and ordered something to eat. After almost half an hour, when Ada started feeling normal, she narrated the entire incident to Sheetal.

"This is pathetic, the bloody rassa!" uttered Sheetal, aghast at what she heard. But, at the same time, she also realised that the professor under whom the research fellow was employed was a reputed and powerful one. In fact, she had heard that the professor's recommendation paved a sure-shot entry into foreign universities for higher studies.

"Don't worry, Ada. We will teach this rassa *a good lesson. For now, you take some rest. I will take you to the*

hostel. I will meet you in the evening. Let's meet the happi first." Sheetal stood up, hinting Ada to follow.

In her hostel room, Ada just kept tossing in her bed, the pictures of the incident flashing before her. On an impulse, she texted Darsh, asking him to meet urgently.

Ada was back in the same Nescafe, a few metres away from the building where she was molested for the first time in her life. Darsh was sitting next to him. They have been in a relationship for almost six months now.

"And you just walked away? You should have thrashed him. Bloody rassa!" said Darsh, seething with anger.

"I was frozen, Darsh. My first instinct was just to run away." Tears started trickling down Ada's cheeks.

Darsh consoled her. "I understand. It's fine. Now, what do you want to do? Complaint to the institute or FIR?"

"I want to slap him first," said Ada, watching her teardrop falling on her blue jeans and spreading in a circular patch.

Darsh fell silent for a moment. He also saw the patch spreading, coming to rest, then spreading again when joined by another teardrop.

Darsh stood up abruptly. "Let's go," he announced.

Ada looked at him quizzically.

"You will slap him. Then we will file a complaint or FIR, or whatever needs to be done."

Ada didn't protest. She wanted to heal herself. She stood up and followed Darsh.

What happened next didn't take more than five minutes. They walked up to the electrical department. He parked his bicycle in the parking area. One flight of stairs and both were standing a few feet away from the research fellow's room.

He looked into her eyes. She nodded; she would go alone. After all, healing is a solo journey.

She entered the room. The research fellow was sitting with someone. He looked at her and smiled, "Do you want to take more exams?"

She didn't respond; kept staring at him blankly. She turned her gaze to his fingers, resting on the table, fiddling with a pen.

"What brought you here?" He felt uneasy with her stare.

Smack!

Ada rolled in her chair, the sound of slap reverberating in her head. She couldn't muster the courage to go down the memory lane any further. The lane was treacherous, and Darsh's company was the only solace for her. She had filed a case with the Internal Complaints Committee, which was an internal body set up by the institute to look into harassment cases. The committee initially ruled in favour of Ada. However, the research fellow challenged the ruling. A High Court judge was subsequently appointed to look into the case, who declared it to be inconclusive. The fellow got away scot-free. However, he was suspended by his department for 4 months. Unsatisfied, Ada wanted to challenge the court verdict. But this time, she was dissuaded by Darsh. Not because he didn't trust Ada but because he felt that it would adversely affect her academics and probably her career. Ada had to finally give up.

"But I will not give up this time," Ada told herself, clenching her fist. She threw a glance at the person sleeping next to her. It was hard to put Amrita to sleep. She had been crying inconsolably since the moment she stepped into Ada's room. After learning what happened to her, Ada was full of rage. "The culprit will not go scot-free this time," she vowed to herself, gently placing her right hand on Amrita's head.

She texted two people, asking them to immediately meet. One she trusted more than herself and another in whom she had lost trust. Darsh and Sheetal.

Her phone beeped once. Only Sheetal replied.

***

Sheetal and Ada were sitting quietly. The computer on Ada's desk flashed the multi-hued icon of Windows, the icon bouncing off the edges of the screen. The darkness outside the window was yet to show any hue of the morning. It was almost four.

"Sheetal, I called you because you are the hall president." Ada broke the silence without looking at Sheetal. "Your support will be required. For Amrita."

She turned to the computer and moved the mouse. An image flashed on the screen. A morphed image of Amrita's face planted on a nude body!

"Holy shit!" shrieked Sheetal. Amrita squirmed in the bed. Ada gestured to Sheetal to keep a low voice.

"Who did this?" asked Sheetal in a hushed voice.

"Someone called Tunda. He is from Patel hall and is a second-year student. This image is all over DC++ and probably over Orkut as well."

"God, what a retard he is! And why Amrita? Did he know her?" asked Sheetal while scrolling through the comments posted on the Orkut page hosting the image. She didn't realise that her question was met with silence. After almost a minute of scrolling, she turned to Ada, who was wearing a stone face.

Ada thrusted herself into Sheetal's face. In a muzzled voice, she said, "Why Amrita? Why me? Why any other girl who is harassed? Why? Tell me, Sheetal. Why?"

Her bloodshot eyes didn't hide the anguish that had tormented her for months. In a huff, she walked to the window and started staring into the darkness outside. She found herself calming down.

Sheetal, shocked by the sudden charge, collected herself. She walked up to Ada and gently placed her hands on her shoulders.

"Listen, I didn't mean that at all," said Sheetal, honestly apologetic. "I know you hold a grudge against me. And rightly so. What I had done..."

"What I had done?" interjected Ada angrily, while keeping her voice low. Both were, however, unaware that Amrita was awake and listening to them. "The problem was that you didn't do anything. All I had asked you was to appear as a witness before the ICC. Since you were the first person I encountered after the incident, your statement would have carried so much weight."

"I know. I chickened out. I was wrong. But believe me, I was equally under pressure."

"Under pressure? Huh. You wanted a recco from the professor for your foreign internship. And so, you thought going against the fellow under him would diminish your chances of recco. That's it. Right?"

"Yes." Sheetal didn't protest, lowering her eyes. Truth can be crushing, especially when told by a victim. The only balm to her pain was that Ada was finally opening to her after so many months.

"But I have forgiven you. You did what you felt was right. Maybe I would have done the same," said Ada, again turning to the darkness.

Sheetal, as if driven by a force, hugged Ada from behind. Ada felt a jolt but didn't resist it. She was feeling balanced. The darkness outside was hinting at the arrival of morning.

Amrita realised this was the right time to announce her wake-up. She rustled out of her sheet. Sheetal and Ada walked up to the bed and sat next to her.

"Ada had told me everything. We will bring these retards to justice. Whatever it takes." Sheetal emphasised the last three words, gently placing her hands on Amrita's head.

Ada's phone beeped. Finally, Darsh got time, she thought. She was wrong.

The text was from Saad. *Found Abhik on 2.2. Taking him to his hall.*

***

"What the hell were you thinking, sitting on the dirt road? We have been calling you!"

Saad tried his best to be furious. But how could he be? It was Abhik. After searching frantically for him, Saad finally found him sitting on a dirt road near the RP Hall. Lost in his world. Saad brought him to his room.

Abhik remained silent. He didn't answer. The dried trail of teardrops on his face told a story. A story of betrayal, fractured idealism, and lost friendship.

"C'mon, Abhik! Tell me something. You have not spoken a word since we met. What's wrong?"

No response.

"Okay, fine. I am leaving. You sit here. Be happy in your own world!" Saad was genuinely furious this time. He stood up.

"No, no!" Abhik jumped out of his seat and held Saad's hands. "Don't leave me!"

The thought of another friend leaving rattled Abhik. His vulnerability turned into a stream of silent tears.

Saad placed his hands on Abhik's. "Hey, it's alright. I was just…Now tell me what happened?"

"I was wrong, Saad. I was wrong all this while. I have failed. Worse, I have lost my friend. I was wrong," replied Abhik in a hoarse voice.

Saad sat next to him.

"Hmm…right and wrong." Saad heaved a sigh. He felt a sense of déjà vu.

CHAPTER TEN

Corruption, rather than its news, has the power to bring people together. Everyone feels that one is being cheated by those in higher power. The ensuing uproar, however short-lived, can disrupt the status quo. The Awaaz article achieved something similar on campus. It made the students feel cheated, especially those who couldn't get entry to the Star Nite at SF. They couldn't accept the fact that money was splurged on parties in Kolkata while they struggled with their canteen dues. Few of them assumed the role of vigilante, unearthing more evidence against the SF team and writing letters to the administration, demanding action. The Orkut page of Awaaz was inundated with vile comments, cursing the SF team for usurping the funds. It was only when the morphed image of Amrita surfaced that the campus was distracted.

The core team of SF met and decided to issue a rebuttal through Scholar's Avenue. Divakar wrote a long piece, refuting all the allegations one by one and harshly condemning Awaaz for their sloppy journalism. He even suggested an official complaint to the administration. Given that he was an insider, he could have easily convinced the Director to take action against Awaaz. But he also knew that Prof. Tiwari, a die-hard fan of

Hindi and who was in an influential position in the administration, would never let the magazine shut. At most, Awaaz's team will be given a warning. Later, Divakar addressed the entire SF team, demotivated by the entire incident, on the Gymkhana roof.

"This is not the first time we have faced such baseless allegations. And this will not be the last time. We work hard, so we party hard. We are not like those lazy, armchair, shitty journos who write without moving their muscles to find the truth. All they do is cook up imaginary stories. So, my countrymen, don't be disheartened a bit. Remember, what we had achieved no one had before was the biggest SF in the history of KGP! Naturally, there will be some naysayers. Awaaz is one of them. But they are not the bloody voice of KGP. They are just a cheap-publicity-seeking magazine. Nothing more, nothing less. And I will make sure that they are punished for their act. They will be doomed!" Divakar raised his voice cautiously in the end.

The speech did achieve its objectives to some extent. Soothing the bruised dignity of the second-years, the new entrants, and the bruised egos of the third-years, the old-timers.

Divakar took the visibly upset Darsh to the side, overlooking the lake. The placid water irritated Darsh.

"I know it must be hard on you; it's going to impact your campaign. That's why I am serious about taking it to the Director. No one can write against anyone just on his whims and fancies. But I know your good friend is involved here. So, I thought I would check with you," said Divakar.

Darsh remained silent. He so badly wanted to agitate the water. "Leave him. His conscience will punish him," he replied meekly.

Divakar patted on Darsh's back. "Hmm...but I would say whatever happened was good. Now you know who your friends are and who your foes are. In politics, it's a blessing to recognise them early on. But remember, the news doesn't die easily; they have a habit of resurfacing. So, you can't relax. If anything, you will have to double down. And take charge, man. Sorry to say, but don't blindly follow others. Especially those who themselves have never tasted success."

Darsh understood who Divakar was pointing to. Halwai had never stepped into the Gymkhana. He was not even part of the core team of Spring Festival tech festival or any other society in KGP ever. The only time he had contested was for the post of G. Sec, Social and Cultural, two years ago, when he had lost badly to Sabu. He, however, decried the election results, accusing Sabu of unfair means. From then onwards, he harboured a deep enmity towards Sabu. He now pinned his hope on Darsh to avenge his defeat.

***

It was almost one in the night by the time the SF team had dispersed. Darsh started cycling back to his hall, his mind racing with thoughts on what to do next. His phone rang multiple times when he was at Gymkhana, and most of the calls were from Halwai. He didn't feel like answering any of them. He hadn't even returned Ada's calls in the last couple of days, every time messaging that he was busy with the campaign. He was trying hard to retreat into a shell. Hadn't Divakar dragged him out of his room, he would not have bothered to attend today's SF meeting. And now he was feeling thankful to Divakar. *Take charge, man.* Divakar's words echoed in his head. *I will not let anyone come between me and my ambitions.* He recalled his vow. While taking the turn at the PAN loop, he saw Saad cycling with someone riding a pillion. "Saad! At this time! He's not really a night owl!" he thought. He almost raised his hands to wave at Saad but froze when he realised that the pillion rider was none other than Abhik. The light from the street pole lit half of Abhik's face, his other half consumed by darkness. The two cycles rode past each other in complete silence. Darsh repeated his vow.

Darsh found the door of his room ajar. Probably, he left his room unlocked.

"Are you not checking your phone nowadays?"

A voice boomed from inside the room. Halwai and Chimney were sitting on his bed.

Take charge, man. He heard himself saying.

"I was at the Gymkhana, attending the SF meeting. The phone was in silent mode," he said calmly.

"Bullshit! We had decided to meet tonight. We have been waiting for you for hours." Halwai was furious, his voice raised.

"And what makes you think I was goofing around in the Gymkhana?" retorted Darsh, his voice a notch higher than Halwai's. Silence followed. Halwai felt something odd.

Darsh continued, "Divakar and I were planning to complain against Awaaz and bring it down. That will send a strong message across the campus, affirming my credibility." Darsh started lowering his voice. He knew that he had taken charge, and after all, Halwai was his senior.

Chimney tried to defuse the tension in the air. "We are glad that you are taking the initiative. What Halwai was trying to say was..."

"Look Chimney," interrupted Darsh, "And Halwai. I am more tense than both of you. Not only is my campaign sabotaged but I have been backstabbed by my best friend. So, please don't be under any impression that I am going to sit silent. If anything, I will double down."

Darsh thumped hard on his desk, toppling the photo frame. Darsh threw a puzzled look at the frame. He was sure he never picked it from where he threw it. Chimney put the frame back in its original position, then folding his hands in a namaste to show his respect for those in the photo. Darsh understood who the culprit was.

"Parents!" Chimney grinned at Darsh, again folding his hands respectfully.

Halwai felt like a father whose son had grown-up enough to make his own decisions. But he soon realised that if the father had to be in the game, he would have to befriend his grown-up son.

"Darsh, I am also happy that you are taking the initiative. Hope to see more coming from you. But let's respect each other's time. Shall we meet tomorrow without fail?"

Halwai got up from the bed and walked towards the door. Darsh nodded. He knew that rebellion is not always the right way. Sometimes you have to play by rules to take control.

After they left, Darsh's phone beeped. *Need to meet urgently. Don't ignore me, pls.* The message from Ada read. Reluctant to reply, he flung his phone on the bed. No sooner than the phone landed, it started ringing. It was Ada only. He huffed but decided to take the call.

"Hi Ada, sorry I have been busy…" Darsh started explaining.

"It's alright, Darsh. I can imagine. But I need your help. Can you meet me tomorrow somehow?"

Darsh was distracted by the noise in her background. *Where is she at this time?* Some voices sound familiar to him. *Saad? Abhik?*

"Can we meet, Darsh?" she repeated her question.

"Yes, we can. I will message you."

He disconnected. *What are Saad and Abhik doing with Ada at such late hours*, his mind started racing. *Something is again cooking up, I need to be in control*, he told himself.

***

"But how do we know that Tunda is the culprit?" Saad raised a question directed at Amrita.

It has been an hour since Amrita, Ada, Sheetal, Saad, and Abhik met at the foyer of the Vikramshila building, far away from the humdrum of the 2.2. Amrita was not convinced about involving more people. Ada reasoned that Abhik could make her case stronger by reporting the incident in Awaaz. It would help when they would approach the Internal Complaints Committee. Sheetal agreed. Ada immediately called Abhik on his phone. But he didn't respond. After his idealism was badly wounded, he wanted to pass the baton of Awaaz to Yousuf and Dhiru. Both dissuaded him, however, from doing so. *It was a time to rise from ashes*, they argued to him.

Ada had not really managed to meet or talk to Abhik after she got the text from Saad. She had instinctively felt that something was not right with Abhik. But she had no time to inquire then. She finally requested Saad to bring Abhik anyhow. He dragged Abhik out of his room and carried him to the foyer on his bicycle. Ada, Sheetal, and Amrita were waiting for them. A gloomy Abhik confirmed Ada's suspicion. *Whatever follows, promise me that we will be friends. I can't lose another one.* Ada recalled. But she needed to focus on the task at hand. She narrated Amrita's case to Abhik and Saad. That was when Saad raised his question.

Amrita winced at the question. The agony of going it over again and again. Ada sensed her irritation and jumped in.

"The boy had sent the morphed photo to Amrita before putting it on DC."

"And why would he do that?" asked Saad.

"Because it was his way to threaten her. Well, he had been after her, asking for a date. But Amrita had been avoiding him. So, he asked her to choose - honour or date?"

Ada looked at both Saad and Abhik and continued, "Look, we have no doubt that the culprit is this, Tunda. And we need your help. Abhik, especially yours. We want this to be out in Awaaz tomorrow. This will strengthen our case before the ICC. And more importantly, teach the bastard a good lesson!"

Abhik meekly said, "We are already under fire. I don't know..."

"I don't care, Abhik," interjected Ada firmly, "I don't care if you are under fire for speaking the truth. I don't care if you will again be under fire for writing this story. That's why you started Awaaz. Isn't it? Ignore the rebuttals. I know it's tough….to lose friends. But in the end, you are doing what is right. At least right…"

The last few words escaped Ada softly, "….in the moment."

Abhik wanted to shout at the top of his lungs. *I am not right. It was not the complete truth.* But he couldn't. Saad knew his dilemma. He gently pressed his hands on Abhik's shoulders, expressing his solidarity.

Ada almost folded her hands. "Abhik, we need you. We really need you."

Abhik looked at Ada. *I can't lose another one.* "I will do it," he promised. Something struck him. "Tunda? The name sounds familiar."

"Yes, he is from your hall," said Sheetal.

"Okay. But there is something more to it. Where have I heard his name? Where…where?"

"Rhymes with the movie *Gunda*," said Saad, trying to lighten the atmosphere. The movie had a cult following.

Abhik snapped his fingers. "Yes, I now remember. He is part of Darsh's campaign team."

Ada beamed with delight. "Better. I am meeting Darsh tomorrow. I will press upon him." She looked at everyone. "Folks, we need to bring this bastard to justice. I have faced it once. I can't see it happening again before my eyes."

Saad stood up. "We are with you, Amrita. However hard and long the battle is, we are there. I know

I belong to the same breed that has done this to you. But the same breed needs to be taught, to be sensitised. Just mugging up and securing high ranks in JEE doesn't make us a good *man*. It may get us a good job and good money. Put us on a high pedestal in society. But is that it? What about respecting others? Listening to others, understanding others? Who will teach them? Teach us?" He stopped. To ensure that his own pain didn't spill over. The pain of not being respected by others.

No one spoke a word. Utter silence. The silence of pain, of loss, which everyone carried within and was trying to overcome.

Ada had never seen this side of Saad. The vocal side. They advocate for the right things. She always saw him as someone to be protected, from the shrewdness of the world. A new-found respect for him grew inside her.

Amrita's eyes were moist. She had grossly misunderstood Saad when he hurled the question at her. Not everyone is the same, she made a note to herself.

"Thank you, Saad. For saying those words," said Sheetal. "It means a lot to us. I am sure if we have people like you with us, we will win."

With her last word, she thrusted her palm, inviting others to join. One by one, all palms joined and heaped up, Amrita's on the top.

***

"Remember last time when we three walked together on 2.2."

Ada, Saad, and Abhik were ambling on the 2.2, close to the SN Hall. After their meeting, Sheetal and Amrita left for the hall. Ada took this opportunity to spend some time with his friends. It had been long, she realised, that they had been together.

"On Darsh's birthday," replied Saad.

"Yes. And Abhik, you remember, you had teased me that day. So, the treat is due," she chuckled.

But no response came from Abhik. He was lost.

"Okay. What is it, Abhik?" Ada stopped, bringing her bicycle to a halt. The silence from Abhik was unbearable. She continued, "I know you and Darsh are going through a rough patch. He would have gotten mad at you after reading your article. His image has been hit, no doubt. And so, his campaign. But it's just a matter of time before he realises that what you had done was ... You were bringing out the truth."

"NO." Abhik almost shrieked, his body shaking.

Saad gently placed his hand on Abhik's shoulders. "Relax, Abhik."

Ada felt bad for inquiring.

"I didn't bring out the truth, Ada. In fact, I killed it."

Saad tried to pacify him. "You can let it go for now. We can discuss it later."

Abhik ignored him and continued. He glanced at the road leading to the RP Hall. How furiously he was cycling on that road that night. How he glided the stairs leading to Rajat's room. He stood at the door absolutely still, listening to Rajat, Sabu, and Mahe and how their roaring laughter shattered his world of right and wrong, how his trust was shredded, thread by thread. How he walked aimlessly on the 2.2 after that. And how Saad picked him up, literally and spiritually.

He shared everything with Ada.

The balance. Ada drew in a sharp breath. *Abhik himself is moving towards balance. Only a balanced person can balance others.*

"That's why I told you that we are under fire. And I am not sure whether we should do other … unverified story," said Abhik, hesitatingly.

Ada did a double take. "Unverified! We have all the evidence, Abhik. The Gtalk messages to Amrita, the morphed image before it went on DC. What else do you want?"

Abhik knew that she would be irritated. But kept his calm. He softly said, "But as a rule, I will have to reach out to the person against whom we are alleging. I will need his side of the story as well."

"Yes, by all means. Please do that. But my only request is to do it asap. I know the pace at which ICC works. I don't want the case to be dragged to the next semester," said Ada, sounding a little impatient.

Abhik looked at both Ada and Saad and said in an apologetic tone, "There is another minor problem. Our next print edition is due next month."

"Easy problem!" jumped in Saad. "Put it on your Orkut page; there is a good following there. In fact, it's high time that you create an online edition of Awaaz. Soon, everyone will be reading online only. No paper. No cost for you. And then you will become," he took a dramatic pause, "Tech Awaaz. The worthy magazine of KGP!"

A smile erupted on Ada's and Abhik's faces, soon turning into laughter. Friends are a true blessing. A relieved Abhik wrapped his hand around Saad's neck, pulling him closer. "*Saale,* you will make me tech?"

Saad raised his right hand, waving at Ada. "Save me, Ada, from this Patelian."

Ada smiled at the bonhomie between the two. She sorely missed someone!

After the friendship drama was over, Ada looked at Saad, her eyes filled with admiration. "You are a real problem-solver, Saad. Where were you till now?"

Saad skipped a beat, his eyeballs nervously dodging her gaze.

Abhik came to his rescue. "Well, he was here only! I guess we never saw him."

CHAPTER ELEVEN

"Is this an act of redemption?"

Yousuf's question, plainly put, made Abhik and Dhiru look at him. They were sitting on rickety plastic stools at Chedi's, which scratched against the soil as they shifted. While strolling on the 2.2 with Ada and Saad, Abhik had messaged his Awaaz fellows to meet at Chedi's. He knew that if the story was to be out, it had to be done at lightning speed. Something that Abhik was great at. Over several cups of chai and Tinku, Abhik brought them to speed. They were discussing who would approach Tunda when Yousuf dropped his soul-searching question.

Abhik knew he had to answer. "It is, personally, for me. I know you had warned me. Many times. But my faith in people blinds me to their follies." He turned his gaze down. A discarded smouldering cigarette lying in the dirt caught his attention.

Yousuf put his hands over Abhik's. "It's not your faith in people, Abhik. It's your faith in idealism. You have drawn a clear line between right and wrong. You see people either on one side or the other. But that's not the case. People can switch sides if they are not given respect. Suppose they are not able to achieve their ambitions if they feel betrayed. That's human.

As the founder of Awaaz, you should have seen all of us as mere *humans*. Not an idealist. You can't impose your own ideals upon anyone."

Yousuf was direct. He was sharp, his words searing. Like the smouldering embers of the cigarette, which still had Abhik's attention.

Yousuf squeezed Abhik's hands. He realised that he might have gone a little too far. He cordially declared, "But whatever has happened, has happened. If it's a redemption, let it be. And it's not only for you. It's for all of us. After all, we are as guilty as you are."

Dhiru jumped in. "Yes, Abhik. We are equally guilty. And we will rebuild Awaaz together. Rise from the ashes." He placed his hands on Yousuf's.

A smile erupted on all three faces. Shahrukh announced the arrival of another round of chai.

"Along with Amrita's story, we will issue an apology note for our last article on SF. We will mention that since no quotes from the SF team were taken, we withdraw the article," said Abhik. Others nodded.

Yousuf's firm voice followed. "And another note next to it that Rajat is no longer associated with Awaaz."

Others nodded.

Abhik turned to Dhiru and asked, "Can you talk to Tunda to get his quote? Before 10 am? I will start drafting the story. We should get it out by tonight." He stood up and crushed the cigarette with his slippers.

***

Halwai's room was enveloped in a tense silence. An oddity for the war room.

The person responsible for the silence was sitting quietly on a chair. Quiet from outside but trembling inside. Eyes lowered, fixed at wiggling toes. Fingers tightly clasped around the sides of the chair. T-shirt inside out, dishevelled hair. He must have hurried his way to the room. And now waiting for the punishment to be meted out. But the punisher was yet to arrive.

The door was flung open. All the six people in the room squirmed in their seats. The door banged against the door and rebounded. The chair screeched against the floor. As the punisher pounced upon the guilty, others jumped out of their seats.

"What the hell do you think you were doing?" hollered Darsh as he grabbed Tunda by the T-shirt collar.

Beads of sweat held back for this moment burst forth on Tunda's forehead. He had visualised this moment many times. First, when Dhiru called him, last night asking for a quote, he clearly refused. Second, when he shared about Dhiru's call with Halwai, he was, in turn, asked to meet immediately. Third, when he saw the morphed image of Amrita on his computer as he was about to put it to sleep. Fourth, while he was rushing to Halwai's room. And so on. But no visualisation could have prepared him for the ferocity of this onslaught. By someone who was driven by a burning ambition, was betrayed, and was taking control.

"Hey, easy, easy…" Halwai grabbed Darsh's arm, pulling it back. "Let him go, Darsh. We will manage it."

Darsh let loose his grip suddenly, thrusting Tunda backward. The chair screeched again as Tunda tried to regain his balance.

Turning to Halwai, Darsh asked, "What manage, Halwai? I am already in a soup. And if Awaaz publishes another story linking me to this bloody…I will be ruined. My campaign will be ruined."

"But why will they link Tunda to you?" asked Halwai, genuinely curious.

"Because they are bloody after me. Don't you see that?"

"Calm down, Darsh. They will not do anything like this. Rajat has been fired from Awaaz. He was the one who was scheming against you, at the behest of Sabu. Abhik and others are sensible, I am sure."

"I wish," mumbled Darsh, throwing himself on the bed. Baba and Daroga, who had ensconced themselves in the bed, immediately moved into a corner. Away from the ticking bomb.

Halwai continued, "But Darsh, you, and we all need to recognise that Tunda has done a lot for us. Whatever mistake he has…"

"Mistake!" bellowed Darsh. "It's a crime. Horrendous crime. And whatever he has done. Now he has screwed us completely."

"Fine. It's a crime. But his crime has saved you, not screwed you!" Halwai was losing his patience.

"What?" asked Darsh incredulously. "Is it some kind of joke?"

Everyone in the room waited for Halwai to respond with bated breath. *What is the trick Halwai is going to pull off this time?* Except Tunda, who had visualised all of this.

"No joke. The SF article was doing serious damage to your candidature. Forget the down-to-earth image; you were seen as totally corrupt! One who will not think twice before indulging in any corrupt practice once you have the powers of VP. Ask Baba and Daroga here; they took the pulse of the campus."

Baba and Daroga nodded. After the Awaaz article was out, they realised that the movie they made was useless. They would have to redo it. And, so, they, without letting Halwai or anyone know, did a quick pulse check by talking to students from different halls. Finally, they shared their findings with Halwai. Had the elections happened then, Darsh would have lost by a huge margin!

"What are you leading to?" Darsh sounded frustrated. It was not that he was not aware about his plummeting image. But he was not able to comprehend how Tunda's act had saved him.

"What I am leading to, Darsh, is that the crime by Tunda has distracted the campus for now.

And tomorrow, when Awaaz will publish the story, people will forget the SF story. And finally, the day after tomorrow, when there will be ICC proceedings against Tunda, and he will be convicted, poof - the story will be completely erased from public memory! Tunda will be ruined. But you will rise!"

Everyone was stunned into silence. No one expected this *trick* from Halwai. The criminal was no longer a criminal. He was a martyr!

"Are you saying that what Tunda did was intentional?" asked Baba.

"Not at all. It was a mistake. A pure mistake. By a second year, who has yet to mature! But now that he has done it, why let it go to waste?" smirked Halwai. He was enjoying the look of the stunned audience. He turned to Darsh, as if he remembered something important. "But we...I mean you will have to use your influence to save him. Save him from being rusticated."

"Not advisable," intervened Daroga, "Darsh will have to totally distance from him. Whatever favour he has done, any hint of any association with a person who is going to be all over the news for wrong reasons, will be a big disaster to Darsh's campaign."

Halwai clenched his teeth. He was not used to get advice. From his juniors. On politics. He had somehow made himself come to terms with Darsh's little act of rebellion last time. But he was in no mood to pander to anyone else. He was ready to crush the tough nut.

"It's not whatever favour, Mr. Vishal Bhardwaj," growled Halwai. "What Tunda has done and what it's gonna cost him, none of us here, I repeat none, including Darsh himself, can even imagine. The best case for him is rustication, and the worst is behind bars. All of us here in the room will start crying like sissies at the sight of a *fukka* on our grade sheet. I again admit that he has committed a mistake, or sin, or crime, whatever label you want to put to it. But he had been slogging away for Darsh's campaign. Really hard. He deserves our support. We are Patelians. We don't desert one of us in their hard times." Halwai paused, setting his eyes on Darsh, whose mind was still trying to comprehend this new twist.

Daroga felt odd. *Why is Halwai so adamant about Tunda?* But he knew that he couldn't relent. "Halwai, all I am saying is that Darsh had to distance himself..."

"Yes, yes, I hear you." Halwai didn't let Daroga complete this time. He was getting sick of Daroga's interruptions when all he wanted to get was a nod from Darsh to his request. "I had spoken to Tunda about this before you obliged us with your wise advice. He will not be a part of the campaigns anymore. Or at least not seen by anyone. I am just asking Darsh to help him during the ICC proceedings so that he is not rusticated."

"But even that is not advi..." Daroga paused to change his choice of words. "I mean Darsh shouldn't be doing that. Awaaz will pick up and create a big issue out of that."

Halwai brought his hands together in mocking gratitude and bowed. "Thank you again. But leave it to us. We know how to do our job. You are not hired as a political adviser. You just focus on your fucking movie. Make it better, make it relevant. And both of you can leave now. We will handle it on our own."

Daroga and Baba, visibly annoyed, stood up in a huff and started walking towards the door.

Halwai went closer to Darsh and said firmly, "You have to say yes or no. We have other things to focus on."

Before Darsh could answer, a loud bang on the door distracted everyone. Daroga had registered his protest. The unceremonious departure of the two filmmakers was the last thing anyone in the room thought they should pay attention to. But they should have!

"I will try my best," replied Darsh in a defeated voice. He tried to convince himself that to gain control, sometimes one had to lose it.

Halwai patted Darsh's back. "That's my boy!" The *father* inside him rejoiced. At the thought of regaining control.

A lopsided smile erupted on Tunda's lips. He had not visualised this.

***

The Jnan Ghosh stadium was bathed in a soft moonlight. The ground carried the remnants of the recently concluded Inter-Hall athletics. The pole-vaulting equipment - standards and crossbars. The hurdles used for the hurdle race. The crossbars for the high jump. The track soil, imprinted with footprints of the runners. The landing area pit, blue and yellow in colour, for high jump, with two standards. The sand pit for the long jump, the crushed sand holding the moonlight dearly.

The Eggies, behind the stadium, was teeming with the night-wanderers. Soft music from Champa's radio wafted out of the eatery, intertwining with the shimmer of moonlight.

The steps of the stadium were unusually crowded with couples. They were making up for the time, it seems, they lost during the Inter-Hall athletics.

Ada had been waiting for Darsh for almost 15 minutes. She tried calling him but got no response. Random thoughts started hitting her edgy mind. *Will Darsh be coming at all? He must be aware of Tunda's crime by now. And the fact that the story will be published in Awaaz. His image has already been badly hit by the last story. How will he take this one? As a candidate who is targeted repeatedly by his dear friend? The poltu Darsh. Or, as an empathetic future VP, who will punish the perpetrator, whatever it takes? My Darsh. Or a balanced…*

Her train of thought came to a screeching halt as she felt a tap on her shoulders. Darsh was sitting next to her.

"Hey, when did you come? I am sorry…I was thinking of…"

"No problem," responded Darsh as a matter of fact. "Tell me, why did you want to meet?"

She frowned at the question. It had almost been a couple of weeks since they met or even talked to each other properly. *Maybe it's the pressure of the campaigns,* she told herself.

"I know you are completely worked out. And you may be short on time. But I am not here only to ask but also to give. Give me…"

"You have given me enough, Ada. I can't thank you enough," he interfered with a hint of a snicker.

"What do you mean? You sound like a…"

"Listen, Ada, I have to get back soon. So, can we jump to the main topic?"

"This is the main topic, Darsh," she sounded impatient. "Forget everything. I want to know how you are doing, what's happening in your life?"

She tried to scrutinise his face - half overcast with the shadow of a pillar, half-lit with the moonlight.

He brought his face closer to her, his eyes burning intensely. His entire face was now submerged in the shadow.

"How am I doing? I am screwed. And I am getting screwed every day. I am betrayed…by my friend…

by…What is happening in my life? I am trying…just trying hard to keep everything together."

She didn't react. She wanted him to continue. To pour his heart out.

"You know what is the worst part. This nagging feeling is growing inside that I am losing control. Others are driving me. I am like a puppet. Halwai tells me what to do. The two stooges, Baba and Daroga, dictate to me how to maintain a down-to-earth image. Abhik's stories force me to change my strategy. And now this - a new episode! Every moment, I am freaked out about how to be in control. I don't want to lose control. Not at any cost. I don't want to lose my ambition. I don't want to become my fa…" He stopped abruptly.

She caught the glint at the corner of his eyes before he looked away. After a moment, she gently stood up and walked to his other side, now facing him. His face was washed with the moonlight. She gently ran her fingers through his hair. He felt like welling up but controlled himself.

Both of them so dearly wanted the moment to freeze. So much wished their love to expand and envelop them completely. Hidden. Safe. Away from the peering eyes.

"Anyway," he broke the silence, "now tell me why we are here?"

"You kinda know that. But before that, I know what happened between you and Abhik. I am really sorry for that. Abhik will be issuing an apology and retracting the story."

"Doesn't matter now. The damage has been done," he grimaced.

"Nothing is done unless it is done. There are always opportunities…"

"Leave it, Ada. I am in no mood to go back. Let's get to the point."

She sighed, "Okay. You know what Tunda has done to Amrita. Awaaz will be carrying out a story tomorrow. And we will be approaching the ICC to file a complaint against him. I want you to…"

He interfered impatiently, "I will distance myself from him. He will not be seen in my campaigns."

"Not only that. I want you to help us build a case against him. If there is anything you are aware of about his past misdeeds since you have been working closely with him,"

"Not that I am aware of."

She could sense his resistance. But she couldn't understand the reason behind it.

After a pause, he continued, "But if you want, I can ask him to apologise to Amrita."

Stunned, she at first couldn't believe what she just heard.

"Apologise? What are you saying, Darsh?" she almost shrieked. "Will an apology correct what wrong happened to her? Will an apology delete her image from the hundreds of computers which downloaded it? God knows where all her image is floating on the internet. Will an apology save her from the ogling eyes, who are scanning her body from top to down? How can you even say that Darsh?"

He drew a sharp breath, "That's exactly my point, Ada. An apology doesn't change anything. A damage done is done."

She understood the reference.

"You can't compare, Darsh!" she nodded her head vigorously. "You can't compare. Your political ambitions can't be compared to a girl's dignity. Please be compassionate. I have high expectations from you. You can't be like others, who are in this race for selfish motives. You are better than them. Much better. I have seen a kind, caring, and empathetic Darsh. My Darsh. Who stood for me. Who would stand for others!"

She looked into his eyes, with a yearning hope.

He looked back, his face submerged in darkness. "What's the use of this kindness, this empathy, if I can't become the VP?"

Hope shattered.

He stood up. "I need to go. But I promise you. No association with Tunda."

He walked into the darkness.

Away from her. Away from her love.

Towards himself. Towards his ambitions.

Leaving an astounded Ada on the steps.

For no reason, her own words came back to her. *When you are down-to-earth, I will support you. But when you are up in the sky, I will blackmail you.*

***

The election campaigns were picking up steam. The voting day was less than a month away. After the display of strength in the Spring Festival, followed by the Hall Days, the candidates started hitting the ground.

Amidst all the campaign frenzy, Awaaz carried an explosive headline.

How safe are girls at India's No. 1 engineering institute?

India Today had ranked IIT KGP as the number one engineering institute for three straight years. The Awaaz story painstakingly detailed the harassment incident, producing the smallest of evidence against the culprit. The victim would file a complaint with ICC, the story proclaimed. It didn't in any way hint at the culprit's association with one of the candidates running for the post of VP. It was irrelevant to the story and would take away the gravity of the main issue they wanted to raise, the editors thought. Since it was not a full-fledged edition, the story was posted as a single article on the Orkut page of the Awaaz. A new upcoming social media platform, Facebook, also carried the article. Even though it had a limited reach, it was an invite-only platform. Below the article, a small note carried an apology for a previously published article. The note also declared that the article in question was being retracted. However, the patience to scroll down to the last word and then read the note was rare among the readers. By the time most of them reached the point in the article which mentioned that downloading, storing, or propagating the morphed image was equally a crime, they started deleting the same from their computers. And once they deleted it, they felt a sense of righteousness sweeping over them. They joined those who had launched a campaign to bring the culprit to justice. Some of them wrote letters to the administration, some thought to report to the media so that the incident received national coverage, and some took direct action by abusing and harassing the culprit. The remaining decided to stick to their favourite way of protesting - commenting on the Orkut or Facebook!

How long the story would remain afloat amidst the din of the election campaigns was to be seen!

Meanwhile, Amrita, supported by Ada and Sheetal, filed a complaint with the ICC. Given the uproar, the ICC quickly initiated proceedings; they committed to wrapping up the case in a week's time. Ada's earlier experience with the ICC came in handy. She helped Amrita diligently put together all the evidence against Tunda. Still overcoming the shock of her last meeting with Darsh, she tried to distract herself from the task at hand. But it was not only her emotions she had to keep in check. The frequent breakdowns, the recurring thought of giving up, the disappearance into spells of silence - Amrita in every way reminded Ada of her own traumatised year-old self. Their only solace was that the ordeal would be shorter this time, even if every hearing at the ICC felt like an endless agony! Ada accompanied Amrita to every hearing. How agonising the sight of the offender was, how it could fog your mind moments before you appear before the ICC - who knew it better than Ada! Keeping Amrita sane in those moments was Ada's goal. And she didn't find her alone in her pursuit. Whenever they climbed up the steps from the foyer in the main building to the ICC room on the first floor, they would find Saad standing there. Always. With a big welcoming smile. Before Amrita entered the room, Saad would join Ada in pepping her up. Then, they would patiently wait for Amrita outside the room. In those hours of wait, Saad would find his years of wait come to an end.

Wait to be close to the person he so admired.

Wait to talk to her with no one around.

Wait to listen to her, admiring her eyes.

Sometimes Sheetal would join them. One of the female professors on the hearing panel of the ICC was known to her. Against Ada's advice, she had tried to pull strings with the professor. Otherwise, she was caught up with the upcoming Gymkhana elections. The SN Hall was fielding candidates for the post of the

General Secretary for Social and Cultural, and Literary and Athletics Secretaries. A VP candidate from the SN Hall was something that the IIT KGP had yet to see!

Even though the case looked pretty straightforward, the well-wishers of Tunda had all the intentions to fight tooth and nail for what they perceived as justice. Formatting his computer was no-brainer. The tough part was to remove any trace of the morphed image from his computer's IP. While for a nerd, it would have been a cakewalk, no one in his circle of well-wishers was one, nor anyone else outside the circle, even from his own hall, was willing to help him. No one wanted to be seen on the wrong side. The only way was to seek help from outside. Halwai reached out to a couple of his friends from IIT Delhi, who, in their good faith, tried but couldn't be of much help. The evidence against Tunda was still hovering in the ether. And the ICC could easily extract it. Halwai thought of resorting to an old trick - character assassination of the victim! Establish that Amrita and Tunda were in a relationship. When he broke up with her, she couldn't accept it and decided to malign him. She morphed the image herself and logged in through Tunda's ID to upload it to DC++. Even though it all sounded too flimsy to stand any ground before the ICC, Halwai and his gang decided to work hard to create a watertight story. Darsh was kept away, and his only contribution to this crime was to save Tunda from rustication. He, in turn, sought help from Divakar, who initially advised him to stay clean as the elections were around the corner. But after listening to how Abhik had betrayed him and how Tunda's act of sacrifice almost saved him, Divakar promised to do whatever he could. He knew some of the professors on the ICC panel, so he could pull a few strings. Being in politics for almost one year, he knew the importance of such sacrifices!

ICC, true to its words, accelerated the case. The accuser, the accused, the witnesses - all were summoned one by one. The evidence was produced and examined. The arguments were heard and countered. The stories were served and dissected. The emotions were poured, and...the ICC didn't know how to handle them. The committee sought help from the Computer Science professors for investigation - to dive into the DC++ and trace the image to its source. In the process, they discovered that the image was the most downloaded item within two days of uploading it. In the process, they also discovered the *dark* world of the DC++. The depth and breadth of the *darkness* left them bewildered. How the portal needed to be strictly moderated was a topic for later, they decided. At the end of every day, the committee deliberated on the day's proceedings. While the committee wasn't bound to report to the Director of the institute before the closure of the case, given its sensitivity, they did send interim reports to him. He, on the other hand, was trying his best to avoid any leakage to the media. Soon, the ICC was ready with its verdict.

On the judgement day, Amrita went missing an hour before she was supposed to appear before the ICC. Ada and Sheetal frantically looked for her in every corner of the hall. Finally, she appeared, a little lost, with puffy eyes. She hadn't slept the night before. Every moment since the image popped up in her message had played in her mind. Continuously in a loop. In the morning, she had stepped out of the hall, cycling on the 2.2, trying to relax her mind. When she saw Ada, she hugged her. "Thank you," she said softly into Ada's ears. In reply, Ada embraced her tightly. Sheetal couldn't hold herself back and wrapped her arms around both of them. They were ready for the judgement day.

CHAPTER TWELVE

No one in their wildest dreams would have imagined seeing them together. But here they were. Amidst the ghostly shadows of the trees next to Hijli Shaheed Bhavan.

A detention camp for the political prisoners in the British era, the Bhavan was where the IIT KGP started in 1951. It was a poetic revenge by Indians. To turn a detention camp into the country's first IIT. The building was now used mostly for administrative purposes and hosted the Nehru Museum of Science & Technology. A big hangar nearby, which served the British during the World War II, and used as a workshop in the early days of IIT KGP, now looked forsaken. A row of jails, with the names of the inmates inscribed on its wall, and a big marble stone titled *Born on the Bedrock of Martyrdom,* describing the 'Hijli firing' incident, would arouse patriotic fire inside anyone.

But not inside the two looming shadows. They were, in fact, there to douse some fire. Fire of enmity.

"I thought you would have deleted my number," Sabu tried to scrutinise Halwai's face.

"How does it matter? I can never delete you from my…until I fulfil my mission."

"And what's your mission?"

"Seeing you badly defeated in elections."

Sabu chuckled, "*Tathastu*! You will fulfil your mission this time."

"I don't need your blessings. Darsh will anyway win. Tell me why we are here. In this goddamn Hijli campus."

"Halwai, I was never unfair. And you know that. It was your own people who didn't believe in you. Dallu Bhai instigated your hall to vote against you!"

"Bullshit! Utter bullshit. Don't spin lies. I had my differences with Dallu Bhai. But I am damn sure he couldn't have gone so low. Instigating against me? You're out of your mind!"

Sabu looked at Halwai with stoic resignation. "Then tell me, where were you on the day of voting? Were you in your own hall?"

Halwai thought for a moment. "Well, no. I was asked to go to..."

"You were asked to go to Azad hall. To ensure that nothing goes wrong there with voting. And you resisted. Abhra, an accomplice to Dallu Bhai, offered to accompany you. You were almost forced to leave the hall."

Astonishment spread widely over Halwai's face. *How does he know all of this?*

"How do I know? Because it was all planned. Planned diligently by Dallu Bhai and shared with Nitro, my senior, who in turn told me. Behind your back, Dallu Bhai got your hall students to vote against you. Now, why was he so against you? I have no clue. You may already have an answer to that."

A visibly shocked and numb Halwai fell silent.

How badly I had fought for the post of G. Sec, how passionately I had driven the campaigns, how I had sacrificed my CGPA without giving a second thought...All for one ambition, only one - to get inside the Gymkhana! Bloody Dallu Bhai. Just because I challenged him...

"Truth can be upsetting, my friend." Sabu put a brake on Halwai's train of thoughts.

"Yes, it can be. But it can't stop me. NEVER. Now, tell me why we are here."

Sabu smiled. A gentle admiration for Halwai's spirit. "Because you will win this time!"

"I don't need your permission. We will win come whatever may." Halwai sounded frustrated at Sabu's patronising tone.

"I am not trying to patronise you. Rather, I am asking you for a favour. It's a simple one. When Darsh wins, can you request him to accommodate Rajat? I had promised him..."

"Rajat! He tried to sabotage Darsh's candidature. And you are asking me to reward him! In fact, what are we taking here? You went after us, after Darsh. And here, standing before me, you are asking for a favour."

"That was war, my friend. And I was just playing my part. With full honesty. Like you were. But now, there is no war!"

"And why are you giving up?"

"I am not. My warrior is giving up. Mahe will pull out, he will not contest. For reasons that are inconsequential. And in such a short time, I can't field another candidate!"

"Ha ha ha..." Halwai gave a hearty laugh. "So, that's why you are here! But Sabu, just because you were fair to me in our elections, you can't expect Darsh to be generous with Rajat. You and I, anyway, will no longer be here next year. So, why bother?"

Sabu nodded, "We have to take care of our own people. We can't desert them in hard times. And who knows it better than you?"

Halwai fell silent. The principles. That's what connected the two adversaries.

"Before I leave," Sabu continued, "let me tell you one thing. Just because Mahe is pulling out, don't drop your guards. The moment the news would be out, I am sure many will jump into the fray. Darsh still needs to work hard."

"What do you suggest?" Halwai found himself asking.

"Girls' votes. That would be critical. Ask Darsh to work on it."

***

Sup Dup was an underrated small restaurant behind the Gymkhana. Overlooking an unkempt lake, it was not a usual go-to eatery for the students. For the loneliness it offered, one would mostly find couples hanging there. But that was not why Saad and Abhik were there today.

It had been two days since the judgement day. ICC had found Tunda guilty and given him a year back. The campus had celebrated the judgement. So had Tunda and his well-wishers. Amrita and her team, however, weren't satisfied; they had expected nothing less than rustication. The ICC, in its judgement, had observed that while the mistake was undoubtedly of grave nature, expelling the guilty would have caused irreparable damage to his career and life. Hence, only a year back. Ada didn't want to give up again. She encouraged Amrita to lodge a FIR with cybercrime. But Amrita was wary by now, wanting to return to her normal life. Sheetal as well tried to convince Amrita, but soon relented. Amrita, desirous of expressing her gratitude, called up Saad and Abhik to meet at Vikramshila foyer. It was not the last time that the foyer saw all of them - Amrita, Ada, Sheetal, Saad, and Abhik - together. It was there that Abhik got a call from Daroga, asking for an immediate meeting. Something to do with the case. Sup Dup was agreed as the venue.

Baba and Daroga walked up to the table and sat opposite Saad and Abhik.

"Congratulations to..." Baba started the conversation.

Saad didn't let him complete. "Thanks. But I don't think that you are here to congratulate us."

Baba chuckled, "Of course not. I was anyway not congratulating you. I was saying, congratulations to Tunda."

Saad and Abhik looked at each other, puzzled.

"They achieved what they aimed for. Distracting the campus from the SF story," said Baba, delightfully observing the changing expressions on the faces of his listeners.

"You mean it was done on purpose?" asked Saad.

"Maybe not. Maybe it was actually a mistake by Tunda. But was this mistake then purportedly used for distraction? Certainly, yes," replied Baba.

"It's alright. We are not here for politics. We were fighting for a cause," said Saad, vehemently. Defeat, until accepted, is not a defeat.

"But did you achieve your cause?" asked Daroga, taking over from Saad.

"Yes. Of course. Tunda is punished," replied Saad without any hesitation.

"Haa," gasped Daroga. "Punished. A year back is a punishment? Why are you fooling yourselves?"

Saad and Abhik started feeling unsettled.

Abhik retorted, "You can't preach us sermons when you are in cahoots with them. Come to the point. Why are we here?"

"I will not contest that. But we *were* in cahoots with them," replied Daroga. "Now why we are here is because we want you to pursue your cause. Pursue it till the end, not through any committee but by inspiring people to rise. By establishing a system that would put fear in the Tundas of the campus. Only that will be a true victory for you. For us!"

"I would have clapped for you, Daroga. But I don't feel like it." Abhik sounded impatient. "Again, why are we here?" he asked.

A frustrated Daroga raised his voice. "You don't need to clap for me if you agree to clap for the right one. And the right one is not Darsh, as we all know by now. He is the one who influenced the committee to bring down the punishment for Tunda. How did he do it, I don't know. He..."

A glass fell off the table just behind Saad and Abhik, breaking to pieces, distracting everyone at the restaurant. The waiter rushed to the table. One of the two girls at the table, who seemed responsible for the broken glass, stood up abruptly, ready to leave. The other girl held her hand, pulling her down to sit. It looked like an altercation between the two.

Daroga brought his attention back to his table and his audience. "Listen, Saad and Abhik, we are no longer helping Darsh. We felt morally wrong after knowing what he had done. Forget the humiliation we faced, even after doing so much for him."

Abhik, led by his instincts, asked, "Do you have any evidence against Darsh?"

"No. In fact, no one would have. We are, anyway, not here to ask you to reopen the case. That would be of no consequence. Rather, our ask is to clap for the right person."

"What do you mean?" asked Saad and Abhik in unison.

"We will let you know soon. For now, let the anger against Darsh simmer within all of you. When it turns into a raging fire, you will get our call."

Daroga and Baba walked away. After a few moments of collecting themselves, Saad and Abhik slowly stood up, and walked to the table behind them. The two girls were still there. They sat across from them.

The trail of dried tears on Ada's cheeks were clearly visible. As were the emotions in her eyes.

Betrayal.

Anger.

Crushed.

Sheetal's hand was resting on her shoulder.

With a cold sternness in her voice, Ada asked, "What did they want from us?"

"No idea. *Clap for the right person*. God knows what it means?" replied Abhik.

Saad's eyes, moist, were gazing at Ada. As if trying to heal her.

Ada's phone beeped.

"It's Darsh. He wants to meet me tomorrow," she said coldly, looking up from her phone.

"Whaaaat?" Saad almost shrieked. Abhik and Sheetal threw a perplexed look.

"I don't know why. But I will meet him."

"But you don't need to. And after knowing all of this, do you still want to?" argued Saad passionately.

"Yes, Saad. For one last time."

When you are down-to-earth, I will support you. But when you are up-in-sky…

***

Ada was punching in letters on her phone's keypad. Her contact list kept on throwing names. So many names. Some were friends, some family, some relatives, some strangers.

Does anyone know what I am going through? The agony, the pain, the betrayal. Does anyone want to know? Huh…what will they do even if they come to know? They will not budge…they will not come for me. They are happy wherever they are. When the one I trusted the most has betrayed me. What can be expected from others?

Finally, the list threw up the name she was looking for.

Dada.

But will Dada be awake at this hour? It's too late. He will panic. I don't know if he keeps his phone next to him. If someone else picks up, then…

A gentle knock at the door brought a pause to Ada's dilemma. She walked up to the door and opened the small window in it to see her uninvited guests. Amrita and Sheetal stood there. Ada opened the door, with a hint of reluctance. She wanted some quiet time.

Amrita started, "Sheetal told me about the incident at SupDup. I am so sorry to hear that, Ada. The person you trusted so much…"

Ada looked at her. "It's alright, Amrita. It's a matter of time. What has crushed me more is that the guilty is hardly punished. That's why I was keen that you challenge the verdict. And take it to a real court."

"What would have that fetched? Maybe he would have been rusticated. Maybe not. For sure, I would have lost my precious time here. The rot is much deeper, Ada. A bandage will not work."

Ada shut her eyes and inhaled with her full might. She stood up, exhaling, and went closer to Amrita. She put her hands on Amrita's shoulders. Pressing gently, Ada said, "I understand. I would have probably done the same. I had in fact done the same. Let's leave all of this now. What brings both of you here?"

"The rotten system," replied Sheetal instantly.

"I said this is over. No point in…"

"There is a point, Ada," interjected Sheetal. "We can keep on playing the complaint-complaint game. But if the whole system and the mindset of people are so against us, then whatever…"

"The system is rotten. I know, Sheetal. But then what? We are not going to write a paper at two in the night. The rotten system at IIT KGP!" Ada vented her frustration and took her eyes off Sheetal. She sat down on a chair and started looking at her mobile screen. *Dada.*

"We will not write papers," said Sheetal calmly, "We will write history. By changing the system. By entering into the system."

Without looking up from her mobile, Ada said, "Don't start your lecture. It all sounds good in movies. Changing the system, breaking the system…come to the specifics. What do we want to do?"

"We want you to contest for the VP!" blurted Sheetal.

Ada looked up and stared incredulously at both of them for a few seconds. Confirming what she heard was right. She stood up in a huff and exclaimed, "Are you nuts? Or are you high on something? I have no interest in contesting such bloody elections! Where no one has any conscience."

Sheetal grabbed Ada's upper arms and made her sit on the chair. Shocked by the suddenness of the action, Ada couldn't protest. She found her mobile flicked away from the grips of her finger and placed it on the table nearby.

"Look Ada," Sheetal was staring unflinchingly into Ada's eyes, "you know our fight is incomplete. And the way to complete it is not by challenging the verdict! But by becoming VP, challenging the system, and then changing it. For good!"

"Yes, Ada," Amrita got closer to Ada, "I have never seen anyone as passionate as you. Even though I thought about pulling out many times, you never did. Not even for once. You kept going, fighting, moving us. Who else on the earth could be a better candidate than you? This is only one chance, and it will change KGP forever. For good!"

Sheetal took over from Amrita. "And we have everything with us. A narrative that can move the junta, people supporting us, passion for winning, experience in fighting, and above all, a strong cause to pursue. You know what Baba and Daroga wanted from us. They wanted you to contest. Clap for you. And they wanted to handle your campaigns."

Ada was still. Still like a meditating monk.

"Tell us, Ada. We are there for you. We want you to be there for this campus!" Sheetal delivered her last punch.

Ada silently rose from her chair and picked up her mobile.

She looked at both of them. "I can't do this. I simply can't. Now, if you both allow me, I have to make a call."

***

It was Sunday. The twilight had enveloped the campus, the last rays of the sun kissing the tower of the main building. A quietness had fallen over the main institutional area, ruptured occasionally by the clicking sound of a bicycle, footfall of a passing student, chatter, and laughter among a group of friends, and the tweet of a flying bird.

The moments before the sun would set.

Before the day would end.

Before the beginning would end.

Ada was catching the last glimpse of the rays. Filtered through the dense leaves. On trees surrounding the bicycle parking. At the electrical department.

She had come to meet Darsh. She came earlier, she wanted some time alone. Not to prepare herself or think about anything. Just to have time with herself. At the place, which has a definite place in her memories.

"Hey!"

Darsh's voice broke her reverie.

"Why are we meeting here? I thought it would be at our usual place. Besides, the Nescafe here is shut!" he said, throwing a big smile at her.

She reciprocated his smile. "Because this is the place where I saw the real Darsh. First time. And this is the place where I want to see you again. The real you. Do you remember?"

"Wow! You sound philosophical! Listen, first of all, I am sorry for how I behaved with you last time. I was badly stressed. And then this whole Tunda episode. It just got me boiling. As I promised, there is no association with Tunda. I kicked him out of my campaign. And I am super-duper happy. That scoundrel finally got what he deserved. So, sorry again. For that day!"

"No problem," she replied matter-of-factly. "Now, do you remember what happened here?"

"Of course I do. How can I forget? You were shocked. Hesitant to take any action. I pulled you up the stairs. You went to that scoundrel. And a smack!"

"What did you feel then?"

"Me?" He thought for a moment. "Proud."

"Hmm"

"I don't know why we are talking about it. You showed amazing courage that day. And now, with this Tunda case. This whole episode, in fact, has reminded me of my promise to you. To be empathetic. To be kind, caring. And all of that. But for that, I need your help."

She silently nodded yes.

"I am in a close fight with Mahe. The recent episodes have tarnished my image a bit. But I am trying my best to correct it. And I will. What I need from you is the votes from your hall. The girls' votes. They will give me an edge over Mahe. I need your help in mobilising the girls."

He didn't deviate from the script Halwai had drafted for him.

"I will do it. But I have one condition," she said without any hesitation.

"Condition?"

"An apology to Amrita. A public apology."

"But Tunda has already been punished. A year back. What good an apology will do?"

"Not from Tunda. But from you."

"Me?" He got the shock of his life.

"Yes. You. You very well know what you have done, Darsh. It's time to show courage. Show empathy. Show kindness."

"Wha…at? What are you talking about, Ada? What does this whole thing have to do with me? Actually, I am the one who…who kicked him out of my team. Even though others were completely against it. And you are blaming me! Asking me to apologise!"

His voice rose to a crescendo. *The moments before the beginning would end.*

Unfettered, she repeated, "Show courage. Show empathy. Show kindness."

"Ada, you are…Someone has brainwashed you against me." He started panting furiously. "Believe me, I am…I am the same, Darsh. There is no wrong I have done. I just need your help."

He held her hands. She didn't react. Rather, she brought herself closer to him.

"Why don't you accept, Darsh? What's stopping you? That day you made me feel strong, gave me courage. Today, I want to do the same for you. Only you were there for me that day. Today, only I am here. Just accept it once!"

She thrust herself further close to him, her eyes desperately pleading. His eyes tried to look away. But for how long could they avoid it? Avoid what had been their love, their light. Like wanderers who ultimately reached their destinations, they reached theirs. Like wanderers who rejoice after homecoming, they rejoiced. The locked eyes started exchanging stories.

Of love.

Of trust.

Of promises.

But the sun had to set. He felt his grip on her hands loosen. She nervously attempted to hold his slipping fingers, holding the slipping moments.

"Yes," he uttered, his hands no longer in hers. I tried to save Tunda from rustication because he did a lot for me, but I can't apologise."

"Why?"

"Because then, I can never win. I can never achieve what I am meant to. I will be like…" he replied in an indifferent tone. He completed the sentence in his mind, *"...my father!"*

"It's not true, Darsh. You can still win. I will help you…"

"As you helped me earlier," he stared harshly at her, "by not stopping Abhik from publishing the story."

She recoiled, her eyes widening. "I had no clue about the story. Abhik had just told me that it's some explosive story."

"Huh! You knew, Ada. And you are still supporting him. Even after knowing that his story was baseless. Isn't it the same? Same as I am supporting Tunda?"

Tears sprang in her eyes. She knew it was the end. If hope was shredded in their last rendezvous, those shreds were burnt to ashes this time.

"Time to say bye, Ada! The time we spent together…I really…" And he walked away, leaving his sentence incomplete.

The sun had set, gathering all its light. It was on its way to illuminate another place.

***

CHAPTER THIRTEEN

Ada didn't feel like taking the straight road on the 2.2 to her hall. Instead, she took the left. It would be a longer walk. And one that would give her time to herself.

After Darsh bid her goodbye forever, she sat there for some time. Not shocked or hurt. Not broken or desolate. Because a part of her always knew what would transpire. And that part had prepared the other part well enough. Finally, when her tears dried up, her thoughts evaporated, and her mind calmed down, she got up.

The memories, however, were not so kind to her. Ensconced treacherously in the deepest corners, they waited for the right moment to surface. And what could be a better moment than walking on the 2.2!

Darsh entering into the SN Hall, their meeting under the PMT, he accompanying her to the ICC sessions, his birthday on the Insti top, cycling with Saad and Abhik, Abhik sharing about the explosive story, Amrita banging at her door, Saad's passionate speech, walking with Amrita to the ICC…

A fork came in the road. The right one would take her to her hall. But something inside her was stopping her badly.

The same people - Amrita, Sheetal, Saad, Abhik. The same question - what did Darsh say? The same suggestion - why don't you contest for the VP? The same answer - I can't. Every damn thing would be the same. Then why go there? Then where to go? I have not spoken to Dada yet. He would ask me new questions and give me new suggestions.

She then realised that there was a left road too. To the new academic buildings and professors' quarters.

Where will it take? To a new destination. To new people. Who will not ask me the same questions? But who exactly?

She answered herself after a moment of pause.

Rashi ma'am...

***

Rashi was immersed in a book. Oblivious of the world outside. And inside. One could see the page she hovered over, marked with numerous words, letters, symbols, and diagrams. A pencil with red and black stripes, her accomplice, was lying gently on the table. Next to it was a heap of books stacked in disarray. From the titles of the books, one could easily understand her interest. Stories that transported her to another world! She had no interest in this world. A metallic statue of Natraj, dancing Shiva, rested next to the books. Her collectables lay strewn on the table. They needed to be collected again. Some shells and a conch. Dried twigs and flower petals. Stones of different colours, textures, and shapes. A feather in black and white.

A postcard is poised at the edge of the table. It was signed by 'Ammi.' A scribble, in pencil, on the card said - *Forgive! Practice Love!*

The walls in the room, painted in limewash, were adorned with framed photos. In most of them, she was accepting awards. One of them had her smiling coyly at Digha beach. Another one had her Ammi in it, a grey-haired, tall lady with thespian elegance. And the final one had a poem written in it. In Hindi. Titled, *In Aankhon Ko Hansti Rahne Dena*. By an author, Agyeya.

The doorbell rang.

First time. She ignored it.

Second time. She looked up from her book. And hoped that whoever it was at this time would give up and go away.

Third time. Reluctantly, she slapped shut her book and stood up in a huff. The title of the book appeared.

The Little Prince.

***

"Sorry, I came uninvited. I hope I didn't disturb you."

Had it been someone else, Rashi would have been terribly annoyed. But she had an admiration for Ada. For her love of theatre. She was the one of the few in the Banjara, who had stayed over the years. Others came, collected points for their CVs, and departed!

"It's alright. Tell me what brings you here. If it's some script, it has to be damn good. Else, you will see my *raudra roop*." Rashi spread her arms, the fingers opening in a vibratory dance.

Ada chuckled, "No, ma'am. It's not any script. But it's the drama that life is playing with me!"

"That's even better. When life gives drama, turn it into a script!"

"I wish I could. But I am not a writer or a Director. That's why I am here."

"Fine, go ahead then. Allow me to direct. But before that, some tea or coffee? Oh, why am I even asking? I have some amazing tea. It's called Earl Grey. You will love it!"

Before Ada could say anything, Rashi was off to the kitchen. Ada, left behind, sat on a cane chair, and looked around. She had been here many times before. Mostly for script reading or rehearsals. Occasionally for meals. But never alone.

Rashi was back with a tray carrying two steaming mugs.

"Here. Help yourself." She placed the tray on a table.

When the mugs kissed their respective lips, Rashi said, "Now go ahead. The stage is yours!"

"I have been in love with a boy on campus. Darsh."

"Umm...Why does the name sound familiar?" wondered Rashi.

"He was in Banjara…"

"Oh. Yes. And he played this character of a vegetable vendor in our play *Bakri*. Going around, and shouting. *Kilo Panch Baigan*," laughed Rashi, "He was promising. I don't know why he left!"

Ada tried to smile. *I wish he hadn't.*

Ada continued, "If you remember my harassment incident, he stood by me throughout the episode. Supported me, uplifted me, and cared for me. I saw a genuine goodness in him. A courage. He slowly became interested in Gymkhana politics. Now, he is contesting for the VP. And that was also the reason why he quit Banjara."

"Arrgh!" Frustration escaped Rashi. "This damn politics. It corrupts young minds. When they should be admiring the beauty and joy of life, when they should be dreaming and aspiring, they are scheming and conspiring. We should ban politics from colleges as if the battle of grades is not enough. You also have a battle of stupid ideologies."

"I understand your frustration, Ma'am. But I was fine. Because he could have really changed the system."

"But the system changed him. And that's why you are here!"

Ada went silent and kept her mug down. She didn't like the Earl Grey much. She was missing the *doodh wali chai*.

"Ma'am, you must have heard about the recent harassment incident. I didn't want Amrita to suffer like I did. I fought tooth and nail to get her justice. But I failed. All thanks to Darsh. The culprit was close to him. He saved him from rustication. I…totally failed."

Ada felt choked. Rashi placed her hands gently on her back, caressing it.

"I don't know what his justification is. But I have seen a burning ambition inside him to grab powers. At any cost. He can go to any extent to win the elections. He has both sides, Ma'am. A bright one, and a dark one. A right one, and a wrong one. I have seen both of them. I fell in love with one. But I shudder at the mere sight of the other."

Ada covered her face with both her hands, seeking a few moments of silence.

She continued, "My Dada says that all of us have both sides. It's about how well we can balance them. I tried my best to keep him in balance. But I failed there as well. I lost him; I lost in my fight for justice. I lost every damn thing, it seems."

"And yet you have not lost. Yourself," said Rashi in a prophetic voice.

"I think I am…"

"Hold on!" Rashi interrupted her. She stood up and walked up to a bookshelf in the room. After scanning the rows of books for some time, she picked one of them. One with a brown cover and golden letters.

She opened the book and started walking back to Ada. Without looking up from the book, she asked, "Have you heard this poem, *If* by Rudyard Kipling?"

Ada nodded in negative. When she realised that Rashi was not looking at her at all, she uttered, "No."

"Let me read a verse out of it for you."

Rashi, by this time, was standing exactly in front of Ada. Ready to perform.

"If you can make one heap of all your winnings

And risk it on one turn of pitch-and-toss,

And lose, and start again at your beginnings

And never breathe a word about your loss.

If you can force your heart and nerve and sinew

To serve your turn long after they are gone,

And so hold on when there is nothing in you

Except the Will, which says to them: Hold on!"

She shut the book, kissed it, and placed it on the table. Then she sat next to Ada.

She looked into Ada's eyes. "So, just hold on! No loss is a loss as long as you haven't lost yourself."

The recitation by Rashi had calmed Ada's mind a little. But the question still lingered.

"What about Darsh?" asked Ada.

"Balance him, as your Dada said. Who can ignore the age-old wisdom?"

Ada gave a quizzical look. *I told you. I tried and failed.*

Rashi understood. "You so far tried to help Amrita. Not Darsh. The problem was something else yesterday. Today, it is something else. Just because you solved or at least tried to solve yesterday's problem doesn't mean today's problem will be solved. Now if you feel his dark side is taking over, you need to stand against him as the bright side. Only light can conquer the darkness."

Ada shrugged her shoulders. "I don't get it."

"Okay. Let's think logically now. What can you do to kill his dark side? Let's think of all options. And think only and only about him."

After pondering for a few seconds, Ada started shakily, "I can…I can appeal higher up. Probably take it to the court and bring the culprit to the books. And shock him to the point that he sees his dark side."

"Okay. That's a good one. What else?"

"I can write about it. Write about his complicity. Create an absolute rage among the students. That will shame him."

"Hmm. What else?"

"I can take it to the outside world. That may damage the institute's brand. But to hell with it!" The confidence in Ada's voice had gone several notches higher.

"What else?"

"I know some of his secrets. I can bring them out. Destroy his campaign," said Ada, her face turning stiff.

"What else?"

Ada asked, with a hint of disbelief in her tone. "Aren't these good enough, ma'am? How many more ideas do you want?"

Rashi smiled, "I had asked how you would conquer his darkness. Not how you are going to avenge yourself or Amrita."

A silence descended on Ada, the one which comes from self-awareness.

Rashi continued, "Sometimes when we see darkness, big or small, we try to counter it with something bigger than what we see. The darkness disappears. We celebrate. And lo and behold! The darkness is back. Much bigger. Why?"

Rashi looked at Ada intently. Not for an answer but to ensure he got the question.

"Because in the first place, what we used to counter the darkness was darkness itself. A bigger darkness. A bigger darkness can engulf the smaller one, creating an illusion that the smaller one has vanished. But in fact, the smaller one has merged into the bigger one, making it even bigger. Remember, Ada. Only light can conquer darkness. So, choose the light. Not darkness. Then only balance can be established, as your *Dada* said."

Ada asked pensively, "Do you think I should…" She stopped abruptly.

Rashi laid her hands gently on Ada's head.

"Do whatever you want! But first forgive him. Practice love. Because love is light. And only light can give birth to light."

***

Darsh was parking his bicycle in the stands of Patel hall. A straight-handle, green and white bicycle. It was the only possession that had remained with him since his first day on campus. Rest everything got lost or broken. Ada had been jealous of it. *I have to outlast it; I will be with you till the end, not this cycle*, Ada used to say. Once, she tried to dump the bicycle in Gole Bazaar, only to be located by a friend of Darsh later. Later, she came to terms with it. Her emotions changed from that of a jealous mistress to that of a doting mother. And to shower her motherly love, she tied a black thread on its handlebar to ward off an evil eye.

Darsh softly touched the thread. The corners of his eyes felt moist. He started untying it, his fingers shaking. Ada's words hit him.

Show courage. Show empathy. Show kindness.

He stopped. Left the thread in a jerk. He started walking briskly to his room. He forgot that he was instructed to come straight to Halwai's room after his meeting with Ada.

"Darsh!"

He froze. Turned to see the person calling his name. It was Arindam, a second year.

Arindam came close to him. "Darsh, I just want to thank you for your ideas."

He threw a puzzled look.

"I came to you a few days back to get some coaching for the elocution competition. And you gave me some amazing tips."

"Oh! Yes, yes. I remember now. How was it? It was today. Right?"

"I came third. All thanks to you. The way you explained how to project my voice, how to take pauses and maintain eye contact, make a dramatic delivery. All of it did magic for me. Thanks a lot!"

"It's alright, Arindam. I am happy for you." He patted Arindam's back. "By the way, which poem you finally chose?"

"If, by Rudyard Kipling. Can I recite the first stanza for you? Just the first one!"

For a disciple, the joy of presenting before her master is the supreme one.

"Can we do it later? I have to meet Halwai." By now, Darsh was reminded of his meeting.

Arindam nodded, dejectedly. Darsh turned to walk to his destination. Only to stop after a few steps. A few seconds later, he turned back to Arindam. "Okay. Go ahead. But only the first stanza."

A smile instantly spread over Arindam's face. The joy. The performer within him awoke.

"Here it goes:

If you can keep your head when all about you

Are losing theirs and blaming it on you,

If you can trust yourself when all men doubt you,

But make allowance for their doubting, too.

If you can wait and not be tired by waiting,

Or being lied about, don't deal in lies,

Or being hated, don't give way to hating,

And yet don't look too good, nor talk too wise."

The disciple earnestly looked at his master. Hungry for admiration. Only to find his master lost. "Darsh," said Arindam with a slight hesitation. "Did you…like…"

Darsh came back to the world. "Yes, yes. It was superb. Excellent. Thank you for sharing this wonderful poem with me. And your delivery was amazing." He hugged Arindam in an unexpected move. The disciple was overjoyed.

In a jiffy, Darsh turned, and started sprinting to his destination. The master, it seemed, received his *guru dakshina.*

On the way to Halwai's room, the first stanza of the poem played in a loop in Darsh's head. Replacing Ada's words. Bringing a smile in his eyes. Filling him with immense strength.

If you can keep your head when all about you

They are losing theirs and blaming it on you…

***

"This space has taught me a lot."

Ada's voice echoed in the silent night that had draped the Vikramshila building. The half-moon, suspended in the sky, overlooked the foyer on the first floor. Saad, Abhik, Sheetal, and Amrita were sitting on the floor, eagerly waiting to hear what transpired between Ada and Darsh. What they were unaware of was Ada's visit to Rashi's home.

"This space taught me how to wear masks yet remain unmasked from within. This space taught me how to look at the audience yet not face them. It taught me how to play the most evil character yet carry a good heart," Ada smiled to herself. "It taught me that however broken I am from inside, I have to stitch smiles on my face. This space… has been teaching me how to balance. In hindsight, it has been preparing me for this moment."

Ada paused and beheld the space with a longingness. The foyer where she had jumped, danced, cried, laughed, shouted, and kicked. For a moment, she felt that Rashi ma'am would appear out of nowhere.

"What moment?" Saad sounded curious.

"But before that, what happened with Darsh?" asked Sheetal impatiently. She had been trying to call Ada for the last couple of hours. Only to be disconnected every time. In the end, she received a text - *Meet me at Vikramshila foyer at 9.* The text went to others as well.

Ada shifted her gaze to both of them. "What happened with Darsh is inconsequential. What will now happen with him and all of us is of consequence. And that is *this moment*."

She stood up and walked up to the railings. Curling her fingers around the black cylindrical railings, she threw her gaze at the moon. Half-lit. Half-dark. She turned back to look at her audience. She knew that it's time that the curtains would lift, and play would begin.

"I will contest against him. I will contest for the post of VP."

The audience gasped. Not that they doubted the theatrical prowess of the actor. But the unexpectedness of the performance took them by surprise.

They ran to Ada. The girls hugged her. The boys cheered; one of them wished to hug her, too.

"Not a time for celebration. We have a lot of work!" an overwhelmed Ada announced.

"For us, this is no less than a celebration!" chuckled Amrita. Everyone nodded.

Ada turned to Abhik. "Ask Daroga and Baba to help us with the campaigns."

"They have already started. They knew that you would agree. How, don't ask me! They sent me something last night. A sort of campaign design. It says that it's a fight for the good, for the one who cares for the well-being of the campus. Don't only look at the Gymkhana office bearers or inter-IIT or SF core team. There are good people beyond them. They also know some dark secrets of Darsh and can potentially use them in the campaign against him."

Ada smiled, "We are not contesting to avenge ourselves. But to conquer darkness."

"It's good to be idealistic, Ada. But idealism alone can't help us win," said Abhik in a mildly protesting tone. A pain lurked in his voice.

Saad followed, "Yes, Ada. Let's carry the light within. But fight evil with evil. A balance. That this space has taught you."

Ada looked at Saad. *Where were you?*

"There is a rumour that Mahe, the candidate from RP, might back out. Baba told me. It means that you will be pitted against Darsh. No one in between." Abhik broke the news.

"Darsh against me. Hmm. Wasn't it always?" mumbled Ada.

CHAPTER FOURTEEN

History in the making. Awaaz carried the headline.

Will KGP witness its first female VP? Scholar's Avenue announced.

The news of Ada's arrival had a peculiar impact on the campus. No one had ever imagined girls contesting for the VP because they were too naive to strategise for the topmost and, hence, the most complex political contest. Because they were too concerned about their CGPA to care for the well-being of the campus. Because they were too soft to thrive in the testosterone-charged battlefield. It took some time for the citizens of IIT KGP to accept that a female could become the VP. The highest post bearer!

It was not as if Ada was well-known on the campus. The Amrita episode, which was followed with curiosity, had given her some visibility, though. Now, it was going to be the job of the duo - Baba and Daroga - to catapult her into the consciousness of the campus. And they were ready with their arsenal!

In an ode to Tarantino, they nicknamed their arsenal - *Kill D.* Much to the dislike of Ada and others, as it sounded like a great saga of revenge. But Daroga assured them that the name would have no bearing at all on the campaigns. It was more for their creative inspiration. They divided the next two weeks, in the run-up to the voting day, into three A's - arrival, ascent, and assault! Hoping that they would not have to resort to the last A.

The first A, spanning over two or three days, would announce the arrival of Ada in the political arena. Who she was. What her credentials were. It was basically knowing your candidate. An ingenious plan was hacked. They convinced all the eateries and hall canteens, in return for a paltry sum and solemn promises, to hand out pamphlets along with every dish ordered, especially at night. The usual channels of DC++, Orkut, and hall notice boards were deployed. Abhik agreed to include Ada's profile in the next three editions of Awaaz. But as an advertisement. So that he didn't compromise his journalistic ethics.

Once everyone knew who Ada was, the second A would be triggered. What she stood for. What her promises were. What changes would she bring to the campus? While creating a safe environment for the girls was her calling card, they produced a long list of realistic promises that would change the face of the campus. The inventiveness, however, was not on the list, but how it was going to be communicated. Baba and Daroga had long wondered and studied the stickiness of messages. Why did some of them stick forever? And why did some last hardly for a few minutes? They found an opportunity to test their hypotheses while creating the campaign video for Darsh. They sprinkled it with various elements - sorrow, optimism, humour, astonishment, fear. The viewers, when interviewed long after they saw the video, distinctly recalled the parts with humour. Hence, they derived, simplistically, that it was the humour that did the magic. Armed with this new-found knowledge, they decided to create a series of videos where Ada would be interviewed by a fictional journalist character. On her election promises. In a humorous style. Baba, keen to vent his acting desires, chose to enact the journalist and styled the character on the well-known journalist Karan Thapar. The character was named Karan Thappad, and the series Tedhi Baat is again a reference to a well-known TV show. One video every day was the ambitious target they challenged themselves with!

The third A was an SOS act. If nothing worked, they would pull out some dark secrets of Darsh, and assault him. Obviously, Ada was kept in the dark about this A.

***

"Just four days! Since she announced her candidature. And now she is liked by 42%! This is nothing less than a war," shouted Halwai at the top of his lungs.

The recent opinion poll conducted jointly by Awaaz and Scholar's Avenue was the source of consternation for the people in the room. Halwai, Chimney, Darsh, and Sabu.

Sabu!

After Mahe had backed out, Sabu lost his purpose. The thought of fielding another candidate did occur to him. But, for strange reasons, the sheer task of finding and grooming another one felt daunting to him. For a moment, retirement looked like the only option. Ada's arrival created a stir on campus. Sabu chuckled at the prospect of an unforgettable duel. He had never met Ada but was impressed by her doggedness in Amrita's case. *It's too early to retire; the world still needs my services; the* thought brought a condescending smile to his face. He approached Halwai with an offer to help Darsh. And the rest was history!

"And the bloody Baba and Daroga have joined their side as well. What thankless creatures!" A furious Halwai raged unabated. He turned to Darsh. "Tomorrow, when you become the VP, crush them."

"Calm down, Halwai," intervened Sabu. "Shouting and screaming will not help us. There is no tomorrow. There is only today. Let's think about what can be done to stop this tsunami of Ada today." He leaned on the nearby table, resting his elbow on it. With his knuckles denting his cheek, he acquired a classic thinking stance.

Halwai threw his hands in the air, ignoring him. "What more can we do now? We have done our best. Our boys are going to the halls every day. Distributing the pamphlets. I have spoken to Scholars' Avenue to run ads for Darsh. We are bombarding Orkut communities. The Gymkhana…"

"Shhh…" Sabu stared at Halwai, raising his index finger. Halwai abruptly stopped and didn't dare to speak again. Silence prevailed in an otherwise chaotic room. All eyes turned to Sabu, waiting for him to pour his wisdom.

Sabu looked at Darsh stoically. "How well do you know Ada?"

Darsh got a faint hint of where it was going. "Very well," he almost said to himself.

"Do you know any of her secrets which can be used against her?" asked Sabu bluntly.

Darsh threw a disgusting look at Sabu.

Sabu walked up to Darsh, placing his hands on the latter's shoulders. Sabu again asked, "Nothing against her, my dear friend?" A hint of a smile on his lips went unnoticed.

Sabu continued, "This is war!" He threw a side glance at Halwai, who, in turn, felt proud to be of use. "And in the war, you do whatever you can to win because winning is the only purpose of a war. Maybe Halwai believes we have done enough. But to me, it can never be enough. There's always one more attempt. One more. And that can only come from you, Darsh. So, think hard and tell any secret that can be used against her. Only you can be your saviour now!"

The disgust in Darsh' eyes gave way to a steely look. He sat down thinking; Sabu's spiel seemed to be working. He went down the memory lane, shutting his eyes.

Trying to look for secrets.

The moments when Ada faltered, stumbled, and committed a mistake.

Just one mistake. Which can be used against her.

The treacherous memory was on its own trip.

Throwing happy images.

The moments when Ada held his hands caressingly, ruffled his hair, and put his head in her lap.

Many moments. Which brought him closer to her.

Those memories turned into a smile erupting on his lips. A realisation hit him.

Ada is flawless.

He opened his eyes to the puzzled faces in the room. His smile grew wider. Before it turned into laughter, he got up and walked to the door.

Unlatching the door, he turned back, "I need some time to think. But it's going to be tough." And he walked away.

***

Ada is flawless. He started laughing. On his inability to find a flaw in her? On his stupidity to leave her? On her greatness?

He couldn't understand. He didn't want to understand. But the laugh released something trapped inside him, making him feel liberated.

He did the right thing. Not for himself. For her.

She is free of him. She deserved better.

His chain of thoughts came to an abrupt halt by a mundane reminder. He was not available tomorrow for any campaigning. And he needed to tell this to Halwai. He turned back to Halwai's room.

***

The door was ajar. As Darsh was about to push the door open, he heard Halwai's grumbling voice.

"I don't know, Sabu, what to do with him. I have literally burnt myself to make him the VP. And look how he walks away smiling. As if we are *chutiyas.*"

"It's alright, Halwai. If he can't find anything against her, we will find it."

Halwai grunted, "Huh. That girl has ruined him. And yet… I had myself salvaged him, his candidature so many times. Last time, I had to literally force Tunda to post that morphed image so as to distract everyone. He was so scared he literally begged me not to do this. But I didn't give up. I promised him that he wouldn't be rusticated. Maximum one year back. And promised a bunch of things. Then he agreed to do it. Bloody hell! It was a nightmare. I wasn't sure whether Darsh would agree to help. I had to manipulate him. But thank God, he finally did."

Darsh froze at the door. His face started distorting, veins throbbing, fists clenching. He was deceived. By someone he trusted more than his life.

***

"Did you guys hear about the Lallu-Patel chaos?" Abhik asked those sitting on the steps of the Vikramshila foyer.

The Vikramshila foyer had become the regular meeting venue for Ada's campaign team. As the mission of Kill D was entering its second phase, Ada's core team decided to meet almost every night. To take stock of the activities and strategies for the next few days. On occasions, there would be other attendees, especially those canvassing for Ada. Sheetal had created an army of girls for this purpose. The challenge for them, however, was to step inside the boys' hostels. So, they targeted the departments, library, eateries, night-meeting *adda,* Gymkhana, 2.2, Tech Market, and all other possible places. Saad and Abhik tried to raise a similar army of boys who were ideologically aligned and who could covertly canvas in their own halls. Yousuf was the first among them. After these meetings, Baba and Daroga would get exclusive time with Ada. To shoot their Tedhi Baat videos.

Baba jumped out of his seat. "Yes. Daroga and I rushed to the tree to capture the bloody fight the moment we heard about it."

"Tree? What tree?" asked Sheetal curiously.

Abhik smiled. "So, what happened, Lallu? People had captured a tree to put the posters of their candidate. Usually, when one captures a tree, no other hall looks at that tree. But Patel, being Patel, did exactly the opposite. Last night, they tore down all those Lallu posters and put up their own.

And guess what? They also made one of their boys sit on the tree to keep a watch on any transgressor. Obviously, when Lallu came to know, they rushed to their tree. The watchkeeper boy was badly beaten up. Patel's ego was bruised. And then came out hockey sticks and bats. The Patelians attacked the Lallu hall. God knows how many casualties! But there will be disciplinary action. Some of them will get a year back for sure."

"A year back for a fight between boys. And a year back for harassing a girl!" mumbled Ada, but loud enough to be heard by others.

"What stupidity! In today's times when you can do so much online, you are still capturing trees," remarked Saad incredulously.

"Well, more than the campaign, it's now just a tradition being blindly followed. You know how it happens with any tradition," replied Abhik.

"Stupid traditions!" blurted Saad.

"Okay. Back to business." Ada clapped once. "Over to you Baba and Daroga."

Daroga picked up the thread. "Thank you, Ada. We are hardly ten days away from the voting. Our first phase has worked well. We are now entering into the second phase. We have some good collateral created. But the rival camp is not going to sit silent. I can see a bustle there."

He took a deep breath.

"This election is memorable. And undoubtedly it will go down in the history of KGP. For the reason we know. A female candidate contesting for the VP for the first time. But we don't want to make it memorable for this reason. There has to be only one reason. Only one."

He raised his index finger, paused, and scanned the faces of those who seemed to be hooked.

"That a female candidate becoming the first female VP of KGP. Not only contesting."

The faces lit-up. The hands rose for clapping, only to be gestured by him to stop.

Daroga continued, "But the journey is not easy. We think we have prepared enough. But that's not true. I know for sure the rival camp is ahead of us, especially now that the two most evil forces - Sabu and Halwai - have joined hands. We can't relax with our three-phase plan. We need to think more. Think hard. Think better. We need to be ahead of our rivals. Do you have any ideas?"

He again took a pause and stared into the eyes of those comfortably sitting on the steps. The stare made them fidget. Their emotions turned from that of exuberance to embarrassment.

He boomed, "No problem. But keep thinking. Baba and I discussed an idea tomorrow. But we need one of you to *sacrifice* to make this idea work."

The word – sacrifice – was deliberately chosen. To rouse the spirit. To throw a challenge. To invite participation.

"There are only two candidates now in the race to VP. A boy and a girl. Out of around 600 students on the campus, there are hardly 40-50 girls. So, it's going to be a very lopsided contest. I am not saying that all boys will vote for Darsh. But it will be an uphill task to break into the boy's den. Even though our good friends here have some committed boy canvassers, What we now need is a third candidate, a male candidate, who can divide the boys' votes. Had Mahe not backed out, he could have done our work. But…So we need a male candidate now, who will have to sacrifice his time and probably his CGPA. He may gain nothing out of this. Nothing. Except for a deep satisfaction. A satisfaction of fulfilling our mission."

Daroga looked at the boys in the audience. They exchanged glances among themselves and then looked back at him. He understood what they were hinting at. He said, "Well, Baba and I can't do this. We need to focus on the campaign, we are already stretched. That leaves us with you two. Abhik and Saad. And Abhik, you are our first choice as you are known because of your Awaaz work."

All eyes turned to Abhik. The sudden spotlight made him fidget. His face couldn't hide his discomfort. He stood up. He knew that he needed to respond.

"Look, I know, this may be a great idea. And… and this is what is really needed. But…but I can't. I am sorry, Ada." Abhik's eyes couldn't hide his guilt when they turned to Ada. "I have already given so much time to Awaaz. At the expense of my academics. My CGPA is in bad shape. I can't ruin it any further. I am…I am really sorry." He lowered his head, and hurriedly took his seat.

Ada went to Abhik, placing her hands on his drooped shoulders. "You don't need to be sorry, Abhik. You have done enough. All of you have." She turned to Daroga. "It may be a brilliant idea. But I don't want anyone to sacrifice. Not for me. No one should…"

"I will contest."

Ada was cut short. It was Saad, his right hand raised, his face exuding an unflinching determination.

He rose from his seat, walked up to Daroga, and looked into his face.

"I will contest," he repeated, this time looking at others.

Ada protested, "Saad, you don't need to do this for me."

"I am not doing it for you, Ada," said Saad, avoiding eye contact with Ada. "I am doing it for us. For the cause we all believe in."

He didn't feel the need to say anything more. Words, he realised, were useless to express his inner belief. The stunned audience gazed at him with astonishment and admiration. Astonishment because no one expected the *second choice* to make a sacrifice. Admiration because even after knowing that he was the second choice, he came forward.

Saad remained still; his stillness complemented by a serene smile on his face. While he was waiting for further instructions, he stole a furtive glance at Ada. Not to seek her admiration. Not to see pride in her eyes for him. But just to see her.

And what he saw was not only her…

…but a sea of emotions in her eyes.

The moment of glance turned into what seemed like a passing eternity. Their eyes locked, but they didn't communicate anything. They needed not. They just wanted to behold each other. Something crossed Saad's mind. A word. Before he could catch hold of the word, it disappeared into the deep recesses of his mind.

Daroga patted Saad's back, bringing him back from his reverie. "Thank you, Saad for stepping forward. We did think of this situation as well. And we have an idea to position Saad in this campaign. As an academically bright student, who will…"

"You mean *maggu*?" asked Sheetal on an impulse, bringing a smile on everyone's face, including Saad. Realising her mistake, she looked apologetically at Saad. Earlier he used to detest this word. But slowly he realised the futility of protesting against it.

This time Baba jumped in to explain. "Not really. As I said, an academically bright student. A genius. Not a *maggu*, who learns by rote. Tell me if I am wrong? Look at Saad's academic record. He was AIR 87. He's a department topper today. Next year, he may become Insti topper, and get one of the gold medals. BC Roy or JC Ghosh. Or probably, JC Bose? One of them, I am not sure which one. Who wouldn't want their VP to be a *fodu*? Yes, *fodu* is the right word, not a *maggu*. So, leave it to us, how we will position him. That's our craft. But he is the man of the moment."

Sheetal stood up, clapping. Not only to repent but also to celebrate. Others followed.

An embarrassed, and seemingly overwhelmed, Saad gestured at the audience to stop. He was not used to such admiration, such celebration. Not that he never wished for it. But he never had. He felt a moistness in the corner of his eyes.

He so badly craved for a glimpse of Ada clapping for him. But the awareness that the glimpse might turn into a doting gaze made him refrain from looking at her. He shut his eyes momentarily to absorb the moment.

And then it happened again. The word crossed him again. This time, he could catch a fading glimpse!

***

The life of a bicycle in the KGP campus was worth a memoir. The constantly changing riders came in different shapes, sizes, and moods. The various parking slots, where the cycles were parked in all possible positions - standing, diagonal, lying, upside down. The speeds at which they were operated, the places they visited, the care and indifference they received, the occasions where they participated, the events they saw. All these experiences would, undoubtedly, make the memoir a joyful read. But the one experience that a bicycle would have relished the most in her lifetime was ambling on the 2.2 in the moonlight. A companion by your side, and the whole experience was heightened!

The two bicycles are ambling on the 2.2 at this moment. We're living that experience. So were their owners. Saad and Ada!

After wrapping up their meeting at Vikramshila foyer, Daroga and Baba requested Saad to stay back so that they could plan for his campaign. Almost an hour went into shooting the next episode of Tedhi Baat with Ada, and then a two-hour marathon was started for the planning. Daroga dug deeper into Saad's story - his childhood in a rustic village in Bihar, his initial encounter with education under a tree shade, the closest government school, which was five kilometres away, a chance meeting with an IITian on a trip to Patna when he was in grade ten, moving to Patna and staying at his uncle's place for IIT JEE preparations, his farmer father begging, borrowing, and stealing to pay for his coaching, and finally cracking the JEE, and finally his academic achievements at IIT. As he trod his life journey, Ada sat hooked, unnoticed by him. Baba drew a quick roadmap for his campaign. Anyone sane would have thrown his hands in the air after looking at the campaign's intensity. It could have easily ruined anyone's last semester grades. But it was Saad who had gone beyond sanity and insanity. He had only one goal!

"Seriously, why are you doing this?" asked Ada, diffusing the silence between them.

They were passing by the Tata Sports Complex, which wore a deserted look. It was Ada who had asked Saad to join her for a walk on the 2.2. He initially thought to throw some excuse, but finally agreed, nervously. Even though he had overcome the nervousness of talking to her alone, thanks to the many conversations during the ICC proceedings, strolling on the 2.2 with her demanded immense courage!

"I already said. For the cause. For what we believe in."

"Yes. But what else?" It was as if she wanted to hear something else.

He stopped his bicycle and turned to her. With a poker face, he said, "Nothing."

"Not for me?" she blurted, looking intently into his eyes.

He skipped a beat. The nervousness with which he started his journey was now finding its way to his face. But he quickly collected himself. "Well…yes. It's finally all for you. You will become the VP. You will get…"

"No. Not that way," she took a pause, "Abhik had told me." And then she went silent.

His heart started pounding like a drum. He felt it could leap out of his body at any moment. His mind started racing. *What did Abhik tell her exactly? Why on earth did he tell her? Why did he, in the first place, tell him?* Then it struck him. *But wait. It could be something else. Maybe Abhik told her how much I hate only being approached for my notes. How much I want to go beyond academics. And be seen as a cool dude.*

With this new-found confidence, he prepared himself to face Ada. "What…did he tell you?" he asked, putting up a jittery smile. Then, in a pre-emptive bid, he immediately said, "Oh, yes, yes. I now remember. I once told him that I was fed up with acids. Want to do something cool? Enough of the notes-guy and…"

"He did say that. But he also said that you had feelings for me," she said as a matter of fact.

He felt as if caught red-handed. His defensive instinct came to his rescue. "Sorry! What? Did he say this? Bullshit. There is nothing like this, Ada. I swear. Nothing at all. He must be fooling around."

She grinned at his innocence. She felt grateful for his friendship.

"It's alright, Saad," she said, calmly, "No need to defend yourself. You have not made any mistake. You can have feelings for me. Anyone can have feelings for anyone. I also had feelings for someone." A remorse filled her trailing voice.

He felt slightly emboldened. "I may…I may have feelings for you. And this was my initial motivation.

Participate in whatever you are doing without thinking twice. But after the whole Amrita episode and after seeing how you were fighting for her, I felt so lowly about myself. Am I here only because I feel for you? I asked myself. Can I not look beyond you and do something that I believe in? And as you said, I also don't feel I was wrong in having a feeling for you. And that feeling was the driving force for me. That was right at that moment. But at this moment, the right is something else. And I must do it. We all must do it."

Right and wrong. Balanced. A corner of her mind lit-up. But it couldn't wallow in longer as her heart was overwhelmed by what she heard. Tears started welling up in the corner of her eyes, but soon turned into a chuckle after listening to what he said.

"And giving up my grades only for you. Umm…not possible. It has to be for a higher cause."

"You are a good soul, Saad. Don't lose it."

She gently placed her hands on his. He trembled slightly, which didn't go unnoticed.

"I like you, Saad. For what you are doing. For what you are taking a stand. But…" She looked longingly at Patel hall, which was in sight, as they stood at the corner of the PAN loop. "I am too emotionally drained."

She would have contained her tears. But a caressing touch on her head opened the sluice gates of her emotions. Tears trickled down unrestrained. He continued with her hand stroking her hair, making no attempt to stop her from crying. He knew the power of venting; he realised the duty of standing by.

She felt it was time to leave.

"Thank you, Saad; I will see you tomorrow," she said before she started pedalling her bicycle.

She rode into the darkness, punctuated by the streetlights on the Scholar's Avenue road. Her fading silhouette outlined her athletic body. A body which concealed a deeply scarred heart. *Scarred twice*. In the same heart, on the soil of scars, a hope of healing was germinating, too.

As she disappeared completely, the word that had been eluding Saad for the last many hours presented itself in its full glory.

Sada. Forever.

Saad and Ada.

A content smile spread over his lips.

***

Ambition is a fabric weaved assiduously. A fabric that has many threads of relationships interwoven delicately and precisely. It's the weaver's charisma and passion that keep these threads in harmony. Done rightly, the fabric can lift the weaver to heights, protecting her from the vagaries of the world.

But the threads, when stretched prolongedly, can snap. Even one thread snapping is enough to bring the weaver crashing down.

Darsh was now juggling with multiple snapped threads. His fabric of ambition hung in tatters.

Lying on his bed, he stared out the window into the pitch darkness. He could see the boundary wall of his hall. Shards of glass cemented on the top of the wall glistened with light coming from an unknown source.

He imagined grabbing those shards and cutting lose all the threads. Ada, Abhik, Halwai, Chimney, Saad, Baba, Daroga, Tunda, Sabu. All the relationships. And finally cut loose the relationship with himself!

Where did I go wrong? Why did all of them betray me? A broken record played in his head. And every time it played without any sight of an answer, it added to his palpitations. Finally, when it became unbearable, he decided to call his mother. He realised he was the only person in the world with whom the thread was still intact.

Despite numerous attempts, when he couldn't connect to her mother, an uneasy frustration started seeping inside him, a seething anger started growing inside him. He felt like destroying everything he could lay his hands upon. Tear up his books and notebooks. Rip apart his clothes. Throw his computer down the window. Thrash the keyboard. Hammer the table, the chair. Tear down the walls.

But where should he start? His amber eyes looked around for its first target.

The photo frame.

He lifted it high up in the air. In the next moment, it would meet its destiny. Crash against the floor.

His mobile rang. He froze. *Mummy*, he thought. He put the frame back in its place.

The screen of his mobile flashed the name of the caller.

Papa.

***

CHAPTER FIFTEEN

The arrival of the third candidate was not sensational news to the voters on the campus. They had seen such last-minute entries earlier or at least heard about them. And hence, they were expecting something like this to happen. After the news of Mahe's departure and Ada's arrival, the expectations had shot up. Speculations were rife that Sabu had a backup to fill Mahe's place. But after spotting him at Patel hall a couple of times, the speculations died down. Now, one would have to simply wait for the third candidate to appear!

And it appeared!

What bemused the campus was the sheer courage or stupidity, depending on what lens one used of an *invisible* person foraying into a war of visibility! For many of them, it was nothing more than a suicidal attempt. Suicide of grades, the suicide of time, the suicide of mental peace. Not that Ada had extremely been visible when her candidature was announced. But, because of Amrita's case and thanks to Awaaz, she had at least gained a tailwind. Behind Saad, there was no wind! He was hardly known among a handful of his wings - those sharing the same wing in his hall, a handful of his department mates, and, of course, a selected few from other halls. That's it!

As the carefully curated image of Saad started emerging, the bemusement turned into sympathy, verging on pity. Why was a department topper stepping into the murk of poltu? Why was he sacrificing his grades on the altar of a mindless post at Gymkhana? Was he doing it just to embellish his CV, for which there are multiple options? Start a random society, say Technology DC++ Members Welfare Society, and become a president. Why the hell would one contest for VP and waste so much time? No. There must be something else. The conspiracy theorists started sniffing around. The sympathy turned into a suspicion.

In no time, theories started floating around. Some close to the truth, some borne of wild imagination. For instance, one theory suggested that Saad, annoyed with the frequent disappearance of his notes, wished to appoint a set of note-makers in every department, who would then centrally issue these notes to students. These note-makers, officially recognised, in return, can mention their accomplishments on their CVs.

Baba and Daroga, rather than opposing all of these theories, integrated some of them in their campaign. So that the real objectives stayed under wraps. Slowly, their efforts started paying off. The first set of followers emerged. A bunch of aspiring *nahlis* - nine pointers - who believed that Saad would lead KGP to its true purpose - academic excellence. A purpose lost to the pursuit of everything but academic! These followers then went on a mission to evangelise others. A vote bank for Saad started taking shape!

Halwai and Sabu, while fully aware of the strategic move made by the rival camp, were more concerned with something else. Their own house seemed to be out of order. A mercurial Darsh was the culprit. At times, he would painstakingly plan every minute he would spend in a day while campaigning, rehearse every word he would speak, practice every hand gesture he would make, and prepare for every rebuttal he would face. And then, poof - he would disappear when it was time to go on the campaign! He would sometimes speak random stuff in front of an audience. And then, he would go silent for minutes in front of the same audience. He would fight fiercely with Halwai and others on petty matters, go absent from the war room meetings, give incomprehensible instructions to his team, and write unintelligible things on social media. The frustration within the team was brewing, often spilling over in the public.

Halwai and Sabu thought it could be the mounting pressure of the campaigns. So, they continued to stand by him in full faith. Little did they understand that a highly ambitious person could stand tall under any pressure, but even a small blow to his trust was devastating.

For Darsh, it had been a double whammy!

***

It was the night before the SOP box. *Statement of Purpose*. Where all the candidates defended their candidature in front of an unruly crowd. And two days after the SOP box was the D-Day of voting.

Ada was squirming in her bed. The table clock displayed five minutes past two. It had hardly been 15 minutes since she returned from a marathon meeting of five hours. A meeting to prepare both Ada and Saad for tomorrow's event. What would both speak in the SOP box, what were their promises, what had been their achievements, what kind of questions the crowd could throw at them, how should they react if provoked, what should be their body language, how should they manage their emotions, and so on.

She was sure that as soon she crashed into her bed, she would be asleep. Hence, she didn't even bother to change into her night clothes. But here she was after 15 minutes, staring outside the window, her mind swarming with thoughts.

It started with today's meeting.

Why was Baba so adamant that I mentioned how I almost fought against my parents to come to KGP? It's irrelevant. What I am doing right now and what I will do in future should matter to everyone. After all, that's why I am contesting. If anything, I can talk about my ordeal in Amrita's case, and that is my motivation.

But…no…I don't want to drag Amrita into all this. She had already suffered so much.

*Suffering…*A short breath escaped her.

Till when will I suffer? I came here for my studies. Not for suffering. Not for all this what I am doing. But all of us are suffering. Isn't that true? In one way or another.

Poor Abhik! He lost his friendship. And his idealism. How much did he suffer? Sheetal suffered. Because I misread her. Thank God, at least our friendship is back.

If only Darsh and Abhik could get together again! But will it ever happen? Anyway, he is at least back to his first love. Awaaz.

Love! Who invented love? Why can't we only have friendships? Plain, simple friendships. At least, we are less hurt, less broken, when friends leave. But how will I know? I have only lost love, not friendship. Or have I lost both? Wasn't my love my friendship as well? Didn't I confide in him like a true friend? Didn't I feel…

Feelings…

Saad…How can he be so selfless? Doesn't he truly deserve to be the VP? No personal pain, yet he is fighting. Fighting like it's the end of the world! Could I have done the same if I was not pained? If I was not triggered by Darsh? If I was…

A beep on her phone broke her chain of thoughts. She looked at the screen. A SMS. Which she never expected in the wildest of her dreams. She sat up in her bed, spread her eyes as widely as she could, and looked at the sender's name again. It was him.

Darsh.

She clicked open the message, her heart racing fast.

U deserve to be VP. I wish I could have said it in person. Maybe in the next life!

She read it again and again. For a split second, she thought of calling him. But then, with the phone in her hands, she plunged back into her bed. Eyes fixated on the ceiling. Mind wandering all over again. Weariness, slowly, started cloaking her, her eyelids drooping. And before she finally shut her eyes, the question hit her.

Do I…deserve to be the VP? Or…

CHAPTER SIXTEEN

Roads.

What is their purpose? Just to lead us to our destinations. Or to let us find our destinations within us. Just to guide us to the last milestone. Or to make every milestone in between a guiding light for us. Just to let us celebrate when we reach the end. Or to teach us to celebrate every step that we take, whether joyous or sorrowful.

Whatever it is, the 2.2 was always clear about its purpose. It was, first of all, never about any destination. *Literally or metaphorically.* It was circular, as life is, as most of the things in life are. It was about the small offshoots it offered. Small roads that led to halls, to eateries, to sports grounds, to academic buildings, and to the exit gate. When you were on it, you could either enjoy the moment and your company or wait for the offshoot to appear. Some chose to enjoy it, some to wait.

The 2.2, which is usually abuzz at this time, wore a deserted look. The road, which was the lifeline of friendship and love for the thousands of KGPians, was looking lifeless today. After all, history was in the making. And no one wanted to miss that.

The SOP box was about to begin.

The basketball court was flooded with white light. The two metallic flood lights standing at the two corners, as if guarding the court, left no corner in darkness. It seemed the purpose of the light was to wash away all the sins of those in the audience.

A bird's eye view would have shown three steady black dots at the centre circle of the court and a bunch of moving black dots, in commotion, on the steps meant for the audience of a basketball match. A further close look would have made one realise that the source of the commotion was not the entire swarm but a small group of dots, measuring highest on the scale of Brownian motion. This small but agitated set of dots belonged to the Patel Hall of Residence. And other dots to other halls – Nehru, Azad, RK, RP, LLR, and SN- are definitely not in the order of their strength or superiority.

Ada, clad in a white shirt and black trousers, her hair neatly arranged in a bun, and her hands resting on the side of her slender body was standing between Darsh and Saad. Calm and composed, she knew her speech by heart, which, anyway, was not a long one. From her demeanour, no one could have guessed the emotional churn she had been going through since last night. The nectar that eventually came out of the churn was a decision that she would cherish for a long time.

Her eyes met Sheetal, sitting in the crowd amidst her girls, beaming with pride. *I hope I don't disappoint her,* she thought. Abhik was standing somewhere in the corner. He was reluctant to attend; he didn't like such *drama*. But she had insisted. *I hope he gets his friendship back,* she prayed for him.

Her eyeballs moved sideways to glance at the other two candidates.

Darsh, also clothed in white and black, wore a fatigued look. Groggy, sleep deprived eyes, dishevelled hair, crumpled shirt unbuttoned from the top, one sleeve rolled up. He didn't even want to shave but was forced to do so by Halwai. In protest, he left some hair on his chin, resembling a goatee. Whatever be his external appearance, internally he was tranquil. Because he knew that someone else deserved to be the VP.

Saad, a nervous soul, was facing such a crowd in such a boisterous setting for the first time. His heart was pounding, legs shaking, hands trembling. His lips were moving fast, rehearsing his speech. It was far easier for him to face a professor in a viva. His usual calm had deserted him. In the moments he needed it the most.

Calm or not. All three, and the fourth one, endured a sense of incompleteness.

A shattered belief trying to pick up the pieces. Ada. *A sense of incompleteness.*

A blazing ambition, giving up in the end. Darsh. *A sense of incompleteness.*

A yearning hope waiting for someone. Saad. *A sense of incompleteness.*

A drowning ideal trying to surface. Abhik. *A sense of incompleteness.*

All of them had a sense of incompleteness. That's what bound them. That's what binds humanity.

It was time for the three candidates to make speeches to defend their candidature. The outgoing VP announced the order of the speeches - Darsh, Ada, and Saad. The intensity of the roar accompanying the names diminished in the same order. While it indicated their winning chances, one could never know the KGP politics.

Darsh was first to go. He looked at Halwai, Chimney, Sabu, Gullu, and others who were part of his campaign. *Why did you do this to me?* He then turned to Abhik in the crowd. *My friend, I hope to meet you soon.* His gaze now shifted sideways to Ada. *You deserve it, Ada. You totally deserve it.*

He was now prepared to deliver his speech. He threw one long accusing stare at the audience and drew a long breath. A sharp one.

"I don't want to contest for the post of VP. I quit. I feel Ada deserves the VP more. Please vote for her."

The audience gasped. Halwai and Chimney jumped out of their seats, rushing to Darsh. But the convener stopped them. No one was allowed to go near the candidates. Sabu winced slightly; he had an inkling of this coming. Abhik, while happy for Ada, couldn't hide his surprise. He never expected this from one of the most ambitious persons he had ever met. A part of the crowd - Sheetal, Amrita, girls from SN, Baba, Daroga, and others rooting for Ada - broke into a hearty cheer after the initial shock.

Ada turned to Darsh. A despondent smile spread across the firm lines of her lips. *Finally, you are my Darsh! The one I loved. But...*

The convener announced, "Ada, please go ahead."

Ada closed her eyes.

Forgive me, Sheetal. Forgive me, Amrita. Forgive me, Baba, Daroga. Forgive me, Abhik. Forgive me, Saad. And forgive me, everyone who stood by me. I also don't deserve it.

This particular moment - addressing the crowd bewildered by Darsh's decision - had played multiple times in Ada's mind. And she had rehearsed it multiple times.

She opened her eyes. Words poured out effortlessly.

"I also want to quit. Saad is more deserving amongst all of us."

All hell broke loose. Everyone in the crowd stood up. Confused. Agitated. Deceived. The convener struggled to make everyone sit. "Let's hear out Saad," he was shouting at the top of his lungs. But hardly anyone cared for Saad. Whether he spoke or not, he was the uncontested candidate now. People started walking out of the basketball court, chanting 'boycott.'

Sheetal and Amrita didn't walk out. Baba and Daroga sat still. Abhik remained in his seat. All, puzzled, staring at three of them, the crowd brushing by them.

Saad stood perplexed, gaping at the other two.

Ada was smiling.

Darsh joined her.

CHAPTER SEVENTEEN

The house was tastefully decorated.

At the entrance, one was greeted by a multi-hued rug on the floor and a wooden nameplate engraved with 'Iktara' on the door. The living room had only one sofa - a wooden one with an olive-green bench seat and colourful cushions with elephants printed on them. In a place where the other sofa should have been, a mattress rested. A white cotton bedsheet with a big tree embroidered over it and four elephant-printed cushions adorned the mattress. The wall above the sofa hosted a canvas painting of dancing Shiva on a wooden frame.

The greenery in the room added to its aesthetics. In strategic corners, which received some sunlight, were placed houseplants in hand-painted pots. Lucky bamboo, snake plant, Chinese evergreen, cast iron plant, and spider plant. A small coffee table with a round glass top was placed in front of the sofa. Under the table were stacked three books, the top one titled *The Nolan Variations.* The yellow-and-white striped curtains filtered the sunlight coming from the window. The filtered light sprawled over the floor of the living room, illuminating it. The various artefacts showcased in the living room had imprints of different countries, indicating that the residents were well-travelled.

There was no TV in the room. The wall where it should have been instead carried a hand-made art piece. A big square of red cloth with a circle of yellow cloth at the centre gives the appearance of the rising sun suspended in the morning sky. A wooden log with offshoots of branches bearing green leaves traversed through the yellow centre.

One of the corners in the room hosted a lamp - a three feet long cylindrical lamp. The corner nestled a triangular wooden chest with an antique look. A digital clock rested on the chest, displaying time and date.

11.47 AM. 11.12.2015.

Minimalistic and elegant.

Ada entered the room, adjusting her clothes. Her athletic frame was mostly intact despite her sedentary job and frequent travels. In a peacock blue salwar suit, she looked dressed for an occasion. She placed a small crystal tree made of rose quartz and amethyst on the coffee table. A natural healing tree. She had bought it on her honeymoon trip in Goa last month.

On an impulse, she looked at her watch. "Ohh!" escaped her mouth. And she rushed inside. To her room.

She gently tapped at the bathroom. The splash of the shower was clearly audible. No response came from inside. She tapped again, a little louder.

"Yes?" A voice boomed from inside. "Do you wanna come for a bath with me?"

"No. Thank you, honey, for the offer," replied Ada with the smile of a newlywed. "The guests are almost here. So, if you have washed your body from the ages of grime, please come outside."

Ting Tong. The doorbell announced the arrival of the guests.

"Look, they are here. Hurry!" shouted Ada while scurrying away to answer the door.

She latched the door open. Abhik and Darsh stood there with big grins on their faces. Traces of muscularity were still visible on Darsh's body. Despite his demanding job in the oil sector, he managed to keep his swimming habit. A receding hairline and a small paunch marked Abhik's ageing body.

Abhik held a bouquet of flowers.

"Flowers for you, ma'am! As lovely as you!" said Abhik, expanding his grin further.

Ada snatched the bouquet from Abhik's hands and tossed it on the sofa. Her hands reached for Abhik's throat. He didn't protest, rather kept smiling. He knew what was coming.

"I am first going to kill both of you," said Ada, angrily staring at both of them. "None of you came for our wedding. Just called us, congratulating us. And you claim to be friends?"

"We are really sorry, Ada," replied Darsh. "I don't know about Abhik. But I pleaded hard to my manager to grant leave. Instead he sent me for offshore drilling in Mumbai. Idiot!"

"Hey, hey," Abhik jumped in. "I also have a genuine reason. I was…"

"Stop giving your excuses. You both deserve a punishment for not attending our wedding." The booming voice made every head in the room turn.

It was Saad. No glasses and no curly hair. He had an air of confidence around him. A confidence that started its journey since the day Saad was elected as VP at IIT KGP.

***

The crimson sun, visible from the balcony of Ada's and Saad's flat, was on the verge of setting behind the hills of Pune. A clear sky with pockets of moving clouds and a slow-moving breeze comforted those sitting on the balcony. The walls of the balcony had Warli paintings, in red and white, on them. Rows of flowerpots on metallic stands occupied one complete side of the balcony. A small wooden round table sat at the centre. It had ceramic plates with french fries, peanuts, and potato chips. A couple of unopened beer cans stood next to the plates.

"I think we should leave for Mumbai tonight," ruminated Darsh, sipping from a glass filled with beer.

"What? Are you mad?" hollered Ada, munching peanuts. "It's Friday. What will you do in Mumbai over the weekend?" After a pause, she added, "With no girlfriends!"

"How do you know we have no girlfriends?" asked Abhik. "And even if we don't have one, weekends are our chances to make one!"

Everyone chuckled at the witty reply.

Saad said, "But seriously guys, stay over. Else when do we get a chance to meet? To go down the memory lane?"

"Memory lane. Hmm…those good old days!" reminisced Abhik. Gulping down from a beer can, he asked Saad, "What's your most memorable memory from KGP?"

Saad was having a lemon drink. He was a teetotaler. He replied, "Well, it has to be, unarguably, the SOP box. I was shit scared when these two quit. For a moment, I thought I would also quit. But something stopped me."

"Good that you stopped yourself, Saad. Else it would have been an absolute mayhem. First time in the history of KGP, all the candidates quit," chortled Abhik.

Ada turned to Darsh. "I always wanted to ask you this but never got a chance. What made you quit?"

"Leave it, Ada. It's a past now. I am glad that I quit. I am glad that Saad finally became the VP. And I am more than glad that all of us finally are here today. Together," replied Darsh in one breath.

"Yes. Absolutely. All of us are glad. To our friendship! Cheers!" Abhik raised his beer can. Others followed with whatever they held in their hands.

Ada didn't relent. "I know that you were cheated by Halwai. But that couldn't have been the only reason for you to quit. Tell me Darsh, why?" She had now an unwavering attention on Darsh.

Saad smiled at Ada's tenacity. In fact, he rejoiced silently.

Darsh also knew that Ada wouldn't give up. After sipping one big gulp, he said, "My father. He was the reason for me to quit."

Others froze for a few seconds, after which Ada asked, "Your father?"

"Yes. That night, when I came to know how Halwai had cheated me, I was lost. I was already feeling defeated. I tried calling my mummy. But she didn't reply as she was not keeping well. And then, all of a sudden, I got a call from Papa. I had hardly spoken to him at KGP. But he felt I was in need after seeing numerous calls on my mother's mobile. And I don't know what happened to me, but I opened myself to him. Maybe I was too vulnerable."

Everyone was silently listening to Darsh in rapt attention, recollecting their own state of mind at that time.

Darsh continued, "Probably, you all know that he left his corporate job to pursue what he thought his calling was. And mummy and I always equated that to a lack of ambition. I decided that I would never be a loser like him. I will never have anyone come in my way of ambition. And hence, you saw me as

I was. An arrogant and misguided Darsh." A sombre expression filled his eyes, his head lowering slightly.

Ada felt bad for forcing him to recount. She went close to Darsh and placed her right hand gently on his right shoulder. "Sorry, Darsh," she said, "you don't need to share if it pains you."

Saad didn't mind Ada's gesture. He always admired her ability to effortlessly connect with someone in pain.

"It's alright, Ada. It's a catharsis for me," said Darsh, raising his head slowly. "Papa was following his ambition. And in his pursuit, he ignored his family and his relationships. He later realised how wrong he was. He told me something that night. The fabric of ambition can only be upheld by strong threads of relationships. Don't lose them, don't lose these beautiful relationships. I realised, by then, I had already lost them. Lost all of you. I asked him what I should do now. He said that he didn't know that I had to decide for myself. What he had decided, however, was that he was going back to his corporate job, that he was coming back to us." His eyes moistened. "And I also decided to come back. To all of you!"

Ada hugged him. Abhik and Saad joined in a group hug. All four felt complete.

****

Saad and Ada were enveloped in a light blanket as the night shrouded the city. Embraced cosily in each other's arms. Warm enough to ward off the winter of Pune. It had almost been a week since Darsh and Abhik visited Saad and Ada.

"I feel pity for Darsh," remarked Saad pensively.

"Sorry?" Ada pulled herself away from him. "Darsh? You are thinking about him when I am in your arms!"

He turned to her and cupped her face in his palms. "You know how much I hated him. For everything he had. For everything I couldn't get. But after listening to him, I feel bad. He was also probably right in whatever he did. Right because he felt right in that moment. And he chased his right so doggedly. Anyway, I am glad to find a friend in him. Finally."

She chose to be silent.

He planted a peck on her forehead, "I am so grateful to have you." And embraced her tightly.

She smiled and kissed his lips. In a teasing tone, she said, "Mr Saad, I gave you a chance by quitting last time. But not always!"

"Wow! Are you thinking of joining real politics?" he exclaimed.

"Who knows? Maharashtra may be waiting for me."

They laughed together, heartily, before they melted into each other.

THE END

www.ingramcontent.com/pod-product-compliance
Lightning Source LLC
La Vergne TN
LVHW041155150826
845673LV00001B/168

* 9 7 9 8 8 9 4 1 5 3 8 4 1 *